Creative Types

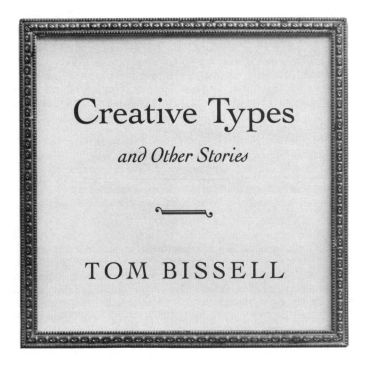

Creative Types

and Other Stories

TOM BISSELL

PANTHEON BOOKS, NEW YORK

All rights reserved. Published in the United States by Pantheon Books, a division of Penguin Random House LLC, New York, and distributed in Canada by Penguin Random House Canada Limited, Toronto.

Pantheon Books and colophon are registered trademarks of Penguin Random House LLC.

Some material in this book originally appeared, in slightly different form, in the following publications: "A Bridge Under Water" in *Agni* (vol. 71, 2010) and *Best American Short Stories 2011* (Houghton Mifflin Harcourt, 2011) · "My Interview with the Avenger" in *The Virginia Quarterly Review* (vol. 84, no. 2, 2008), *Who Can Save Us Now? Brand-New Superheroes and Their Amazing (Short) Stories* (Free Press, 2008), and *Best American Mystery Stories 2009* (Houghton Mifflin Harcourt, 2009) · "Punishment" in *The Normal School* (vol. 1, no. 1, 2008) · "The Fifth Category" in *The Normal School* (vol. 2, no. 2, 2009) and *Flight or Fright* (Cemetery Dance Publications, 2018) · "Love Story, with Cocaine" in *Zyzzyva* (no. 92, Fall 2011) · "Creative Types" in *The Paris Review* (no. 219, Winter 2016) and *The Pushcart Prize Anthology XLII* (Pushcart Press, 2018).

Library of Congress Cataloging-in-Publication Data
Name: Bissell, Tom, [date] author.
Title: Creative types : and other stories / Tom Bissell.
Description: New York : Pantheon Books, 2021.
Identifiers: LCCN 2019056601 (print). LCCN 2019056602 (ebook).
ISBN 9781524749156 (hardcover). ISBN 9781524749163 (ebook).
Classification: LCC PS3602.I78 A6 2021 (print) |
LCC PS3602.I78 (ebook) | DDC 813/.6—dc23
LC record available at lccn.loc.gov/2019056601
LC ebook record available at lccn.loc.gov/2019056602

www.pantheonbooks.com

Jacket design by Tyler Comrie

Printed in Canada

First Edition
2 4 6 8 9 7 5 3 1

For Mina Miller Bissell
and in memory of John C. Bissell

I had become to myself a vast problem.

—Augustine, *Confessions*

Contents

A Bridge Under Water

S o," he said, after having vacuumed up a plate of penne all'arrabbiata, drunk in three quick swallows a glass of Ncro d'Avola, and consumed half a basket of breadsticks, "do you want to hit another church or see the Borghese Gallery?"

She had taken a few bites of her strawberry risotto and two birdfeeder sips from the glass of Gewürztraminer that her waiter (a genius, clearly) had recommended pairing with it. She glanced up and smiled at him more or less genuinely. The man put away everything from foie gras to a Wendy's single with the joyless efficiency of a twelve-year-old. He never appeared to taste anything. The plate before him looked licked clean. When he return-serve smiled, she tried not to notice his red-pepper-and-wine-stained teeth or the breadcrumbs scattered throughout his short beard. They were sitting on the Astroturfed patio of an otherwise pleasing restaurant found right behind the American embassy in Rome. They had been married for three and a half days.

Thus she pushed her fork into the risotto and watched steam rise from its disturbed center. "Think I may be a little churched out."

He snapped up another breadstick, leaned back, and rubbed his mouth. This succeeded, perhaps accidentally, in clearing the breadcrumb perimeter around his mouth. He had small eyes whose irises were as hard and green as marbles, a crooked wide nose, and an uncommonly large chin. His thick brown hair sat upon his head with shaggy indifference. She did not mind that he had overslept or the panicked rush with which they had left their hotel. (The only reason she had not overslept was that she had never fallen asleep to begin with.) His purple linen shirt was unbuttoned to his sternum, showcasing a pale white chest covered in pubically corkscrewed hair. She felt an urge to lean forward and button him up but did not want such mothering tasks ever to fall to her.

He bit the end off his breadstick. "It's not a church, strictly speaking. It's more like a crypt." Now that he was gesturing, the breadstick resembled a wand. "Mark Twain wrote something really funny about it when he visited Rome. Apparently it's decorated with the bones of all the monks who've lived there. Like four centuries' worth. The chandeliers are bones, the gates, everything. All bones. It's supposed to be really creepy."

"A crypt made of monk bones. Why didn't you say so? Let's do that."

His smile softened in a pleased way that made her realize how false his earlier, larger smile had been. "Funny girl," he said. The thing he liked most about her, he enjoyed telling people when she was in earshot, was her sense of humor. He was the only man who had ever said she was funny, and she wondered, suddenly, if that was one of the reasons she married him. She was, in fact, very funny.

It had been a good morning, uncontaminated by the reactor-leak conversation of the previous night. They had hardly talked about things today, but she knew both of them were aware they would have to. It was the lone solid thing in their day's formless future. It was the train they would have to catch.

"Okay," he said, setting down his breadstick with an air of

tragic relinquishment, "I'd really like to see the creepy bone crypt."

She put her hands on her only slightly rounded belly and gave it a crystal-ball rubbing. "Let the record show the pregnant lady would like to see the Borghese Gallery."

The single drum of his fingers on the tabletop made a sound like a gallop. "One way to settle it."

She slammed her fork to the table. "I'm not playing. Seriously. I won't do it."

He was nodding. "One way to settle it."

The man loved games of all kinds—obscure board games, video games manufactured prior to 1990, any and all word games—but he also enjoyed purely biophysical games such as rock, paper, scissors, the "essential fairness" of which he claimed to particularly admire. He was, however, miserably bad at rock, paper, scissors, the reason being that he almost always took paper. She had once been told, as a girl, by some forgotten Hebrew school playmate, that while playing rock, paper, scissors you were allowed, once in your life, the option of a fourth component. This was fire, which was signified by turning up your hand on the third beat and wiggling your fingers. Fire destroyed everything. That this thermonuclear gambit could be used only once was a rule so mystically stern its validity seemed impossible to question. She had told him of the fire rule when he first challenged her to rock, paper, scissors on their earliest date, which had not been that long ago. At issue had been what movie to go see.

Now she said to him, "You do realize you always lose. You're aware of this."

He readied his playing stance: back against the chair, eyes full of blank concentration, right fist set upon the small shelf of his left hand.

She picked up her fork again and began to eat. Probably she would indulge him. "I'm not playing because it's boring. And it's boring because you always pick paper."

"I like its quiet efficiency. I could ask you why you always take scissors."

"Because you always take paper!"

"I am aware that you believe that, which means I'm actually taking paper to psych you out. Statistically I can't keep it up."

"But you *do*. The last time we played you took paper four throws in a *row*."

"I know. And I can't possibly keep it up. Or can I? Now, best out of three. No. Five. Three. Best out of three." He was smiling again, his teeth no longer quite so stained by the wine and pepper oil. She loved him, she had to admit, a lot right now.

He threw paper for the first two throws. She threw rock for her first just to make the game interesting. After his second paper she fished an ice cube out of her hitherto untouched water glass and threw it at him. On the third throw she was astonished to see her husband wiggling his fingers.

"Fire," he said, extending his still-wiggling fingers so that they burned harmlessly beneath her nose. What he said next was sung in hair-metal falsetto: "Motherfucking fire!"

She pushed his hand away. "You didn't even know about fire until I told you about it!"

"Look at the bright side," he said. "I can never use it again, and you've still got yours."

"Please, honey, *please* button your shirt."

"Well," he said, as they exited the apricot building she now knew was called the Capuchin Crypt, "that *was* creepy. Holy shit."

On their way down zigzagging stairs they passed a dozen

American student-tourists sitting on, around, and along the stone balustrade. The boys, clearly suffering the misapplications of energy that distinguished all educational field trips, spoke in hey-I'm-shouting voices to the bare-shouldered and sort of lusciously sweaty girls sitting two feet away from them. She was upsettingly conscious of the adult conservatism of her thinly striped collared shirt and black skirt—she was not yet showing so much that her wardrobe required any real overhaul—and her collar, moreover, had wilted in the heat. She felt like a sun-baked flower someone had overwatered in recompense. How much older was she than these girls, anyway, who seemed to her another species altogether? And yet she was only twenty-six, her husband thirty-four. Two once-unimaginable objects, the first incubating in her stomach and the second enclosed around her ring finger, made her, she realized, unable to remember what being nineteen or twenty even felt like. Looking into the anime innocence of these American girls' faces was to discover the power of new anxieties and the stubbornness of old ones.

At the bottom of the stairs three tanned and lithe young Italian women walked unknowably by. She often felt herself bend away from people who knew how good they looked, but these women had such costume-party exuberance it seemed a waste not to stare. The belt? Three hundred dollars, easy. She somehow counted five purses among them. She hated the farthest girl's rimless aviatrix sunglasses only because she knew she could never wear them without fearing she looked ridiculous. She glanced down at her pink-accented gray Pumas and then over at one of the growingly distant Italian's sassy red pumps. She had worn the Pumas only because she felt marriage should annul the desire to impress strangers, a thought that made her feel at once happy and vaguely condemned.

"Know what?" he said as they turned toward where Via Veneto

terminated at Palazzo Barberini. "Those bones kind of freaked me out. Seriously."

She was still staring at her stupid shoes. "We could have spent that time looking at Bernini sculptures."

His hand alit upon her back. "We could still do that. I'd be happy to."

"No, it's okay. I'm tired anyway."

"You want to go back to the hotel?" His hand sprang away from her back as he checked his watch. "It's not even three yet." The hand did not return.

She did not say anything, thus sealing their hotel-bound fate. The next block or so was passed in silence, and he turned onto a tight, unremarkable side street (if any street in Rome could be considered unremarkable) made even tighter by the chaotically fender-to-grille-parked cars along both curbs. This was as residential as central Rome had yet seemed to her: hugely ornate wooden double doors with five-pound brass knockers and black-barred ground-level windows. The only word she could think of to describe it was *postimperial,* which she knew was not even close to being historically correct. She liked this about Rome: whether you knew anything at all about history, and she knew a little, it forced you to think about history, even if in variously crackpot ways. In many cities, history was a party at which one felt underdressed. In Rome she felt history pressing in on all sides of her, but in a pleasant, consensual way.

"Not entirely sure I like it here," he suddenly said.

She turned to him. "That's not a nice thing to say."

"No, no. I like being here with *you*. I mean I'm not sure I like Rome. The city. In and of itself."

She supposed she would have to hear this out but let his opportunity for explanation dangle a moment longer than felt polite. "Okay. Why not?"

"It really bothers me that everything is closed from noon to four, for starters, and that if you order a cappuccino after breakfast you're a barbarian. And I realized yesterday that I don't like how Italians talk to one another. Everything is so *emotional*. Like those women sitting next to us on the stairs the other day. Listening to them was like overhearing a plot to kidnap the pope. And when I asked that kid what they'd been talking about, he said, 'Shoes.' "

"I thought that was funny."

"You know my friend who lived in Rome for a while? What I didn't tell you is that his first apartment burned down—I guess the wiring was all fucked up—and after the fire was finally put out he and some firemen went inside to see what survived. Exactly one wall did, in the middle of which was this scorched crucifix that had been hung at the insistence of his landlady. There were any number of reasons why this wall survived the fire, but when they saw it all the firemen dropped to their knees and started praying while my friend just stood there. He made the point that you'd have to be astonishingly simple to believe in a god who'd let someone's apartment burn down but magically intervene to save a three-dollar version of his own likeness. He also told me that Italians are basically the most complicated uninteresting people in the world."

"You're being really interesting yourself right now."

"I'm not trying to be interesting." His voice had a real snarl in it. "I'm trying to objectively describe my impressions and tell you about my friend." Then he calmed down, or at least hid his anger more cunningly. "I'm sorry I made fun of your book last night."

Before their argument, while at a restaurant and while she was in the ladies', he had fished out of her purse the travel book she was reading about Italy. Its author was an American woman.

9

When she returned to the table he began to read aloud certain parts in a dopey voice. "Listen to what she has to say about Rome: 'It's like someone invented a city just to suit my specifications.' Considerate of the preceding twenty-seven hundred years of civilization, wasn't it? This is priceless: 'It's like the whole society is conspiring to teach me Italian. They'll even print their newspapers in Italian while I'm here; they don't mind!'" He tossed the book onto the table and stared at it as though it were an excised tumor. Finally he said, "That is, without question, the stupidest fucking book I've ever seen you read."

The book in question was currently a bestseller, and the only reason she was reading it was that her mother had given it to her, just as she had given her (them) the gift of an Italian honeymoon. He, too, was a travel writer, though one who had never made it off what he sometimes called the "worstseller list." He had published three books, all before she had met him, and preferred writing about places, he had once said in an interview she was embarrassed for him to have given, with "adrenaline payoffs": Nigeria, Laos, Mongolia. (His honeymoon suggestion? Azerbaijan.) She admired his determination to love the unloved parts of the world, but, like all good qualities, it remained admirable only insofar as it was unacknowledged.

She decided to speak carefully. "I *like* that everything is closed from noon to four. It creates a little oasis in the middle of the day. I *like* that life in this city isn't based around my own convenience. I also like that people talk about dumb, pointless things like shoes with passion here. And I like Italians. They seem like totally lovely people."

"I guess what irks me," he said, speaking just as carefully, "is this fantasy that Italy exists only as a sensory paradise when it's got all these completely obvious *problems*."

"Okay. How about this: I hated your creepy bone church."

"Excuse me. Creepy bone *crypt*."

"In fact, I've hated every stupid church we've walked into."
She knew she was asking for it here, and waited. He said nothing.
Onward, then, into the dark. "You know I'm not comfortable in
churches and yet you keep dragging me into them."

Five pounds of emotion seemed to encumber his face.
"Please, let's at least lie down before we start talking about this
again."

The hotel was many blocks away.

"Why," she asked, "do you *want* to take me into places you
know I'm not comfortable in?"

His mouth set into an ugly little frown. "Because I think this
discomfort of yours is ridiculous. I'm no more of a Christian
than you are. The ideology you suddenly feel so offended by is
an ideology that would have had someone like me burning at the
stake right next to you. That you can't separate the objectively
aesthetic pleasure of churches from your own—" He stopped
walking. Standing there, he began to rub his eyes. "Christ. Just
forget it."

"My own what?" Now she had stopped, too. They were outside the gate-lowered entrance of a cheese store, the owner of
which was probably off banging his noontime mistress about
now, and good for him.

He fixed upon her an envenomed look, clearly resisting what
he wanted to say. *Religion,* she knew, was what he wanted to say.

He recklessly took her hands in his. When she made no effort
to return his clasp he rubbed his thumb along the valley between
her index and middle-finger knuckles. His voice turned soft. "I
cannot understand why you're so attached to being Jewish when
you don't even believe in God. And why all of this is only coming
up now. Not to mention why we keep fighting about it."

"And I cannot understand your difficulty in understanding

this. It has nothing to do with God and your position is absolutely bizarre to me." With this she twisted her hands around so that she was holding his. "And it makes me, I have to tell you, extremely worried and sad."

Last night, after the restaurant, after the confrontation over the stupidest fucking book he had ever seen her read, they had argued, again, for the first time since the wedding, about their child, due now in six months. They had told themselves, in the weeks leading up to the wedding, that her accidental pregnancy after four months of dating was not the reason they had decided to get married. But it was clear to both of them now that this was probably not the case. She knew he felt betrayed. His atheism was one of the first things he had told her about himself, and once things became serious he had quizzed her about her feelings concerning God. She had answered that she had no particular feelings about God, other than a strong suspicion he did not exist. This had made him happy at a time when his happiness seemed to her a most precious and mysterious thing.

All of that had begun to unspool a week before their (secular) wedding, when she had mentioned (in passing) that it was important (to her) that their child would understand him- or herself (they had agreed on keeping the child's gender a surprise) as a Jew. She could not even remember the context in which this had come up—*that* was how uncontroversially she had regarded the matter. At hearing that his child would be Jewish, her husband had laughed, once and loudly, like a king at some forced merriment, before realizing his pregnant fiancée was not kidding. *We'll . . . talk about that later,* he had told her. She did not let him, saying that it was beyond her ability to fathom how exactly this could bother him. What was there to talk about? She was Jewish, her parents were Jewish, her child would be Jewish.

His position: Jewishness was and could be only a religion. It was not a race, because there were Chinese and Turkish and Indian Jews. He had met some himself. It was not a proper culture, because there were Sephardic Jews, for instance, whose culture was completely different from that of Ashkenazi Jews. He described to her—one of his less wise moments—some of those differences. It was not an ethnicity, because the idea of Jewishness being determined by matrilineal descent was a religious concept. Out came his feverishly marginaliaed New Revised Standard for citation. It was, therefore, only and solely a religion, and, he told her, he could not and in fact refused to live within a household, a family, in which religion played any role other than that of an occasionally bashed piñata.

She chose not to argue with this reasoning, which part of her agreed with. She disliked Jewish tribalism as much as anyone and had managed to escape Hebrew school without learning how to read, speak, or write Hebrew. Once, after a nephew's bar mitzvah, the theme of which was Wall Street, and which her uncle had made known cost $22,000, she had actually renounced her Jewishness (for two days). But she was having a child, and while she did not want to raise Menachem Begin, a Chabadnik, or a Settler, she did want to raise a Jew in the way she was a Jew, the formalities of which she knew almost nothing about. Being Jewish was, in her innerland, nothing more than a faint but definite light, and it offered her no more pride or direction than that of a faint but definite light. His refusal to grant her, and their child, that tiny, private awareness seemed to her insane.

Since their first argument, she had found herself doing and thinking things that she previously could have never envisioned: feeling unfamiliar pangs while eating pork, writing *G-d* instead of *God* in emails, sneering at strangers' pendant crucifixes, resenting churches, discovering within herself an out-of-nowhere identification with a Certain Small Country She Had Never Been To And Did Not Ever Want To Visit. She had no explanation for these things.

They stood holding each other's hands outside the cheese store. There seemed no place for this already battle-weary argument to go, other than deeper into a bunker, where it might just as well blow its own brains out. Suddenly she was crying. His forehead lurched forward, lightly bumping hers. "Don't cry," he said.

She shook her head. "I feel like I've disappointed you in a way I can't even control."

"I'm not disappointed. Disappointment is a beautiful woman reading Ayn Rand. This is not disappointment. This is something we can get through."

"But what if we can't?"

"Then I guess it's a bridge under water."

At the same time they squeezed each other's hands. His brother, a second lieutenant in the Marine Corps, had over the last five years of his eventful service become quite a collector of military-grade phraseology: *unimprovised road, northeasterlyward, shrapmetal, validify,* and *increasely.* "A bridge under water," which a gunnery sergeant had once used to describe to her husband's brother a particularly bad Ramadi neighborhood, was, as her husband knew, her personal favorite. She loved his brother.

She hugged him now with real love, its smoldering edges suddenly extinguished. "I hope it's not a bridge under water. It would be a real blow to my parade if it were."

His arms reached around her back. When he spoke into her hair his voice was unfamiliarly husky. "No need to reinvent the clock."

—

When they reached their room she slept in her clothes for the rest of the afternoon and awoke around seven to find him writing in his notebook. She admired that about him, too. He could write anywhere. He claimed to have once written an entire op-ed in the bathroom at a friend's birthday party. But she knew that he had not been writing much lately. He told her a while ago that he felt convinced "the time for the American voice was over," which sounded even more pretentious when he said it.

She watched him for a little while and said, "Hey," a drowsy creak in her voice breaking the word in two. "What are you doing?"

"Writing," he said.

"I gathered. What about?"

"A monkey with an unusual level of curiosity. This gets him into trouble in the short term but consistently results in long-term gains for those around him. I think this is due to the purity of his motivation, though I have to admit, I'm just getting to know the character."

When he got like this she really enjoyed throwing things at him and now launched across the room her big, supernaturally downy pillow. He absorbed the blow and continued writing. She sat up and looked around the room, which was absurd, beginning with the fact that it did not have a number but rather a symbol. (The floors did not have numbers either; they had colors; they were on Green.) Their room's symbol resembled a Celtic cross. Upon check-in, they had been given a sheet with peel-away representations of this symbol, which they were supposed to affix to all relevant bills. It was apparently some sort of "art hotel," and everything in the room had a gadgety double function. The shower's clear glass door turned discreetly opaque when the water was running. The wall-hung flat-screen television could be pulled out from its steel rigging on a bizarrely lengthy extender arm and angled this way or that. The day they arrived they had engaged in a long discussion about whether this last innovation was "worthless" or "next to worthless." The decor itself was Modern Android, everything shiny and smooth, with drawers and closets that made no sound when you opened them. She actually kind of loved it here.

She looked at him. "Do you want to order room service and do it like teenagers?"

He crossed something out, glanced over at her, and frowned in a hard-to-read way. They had not made love since the first night they were here, though they had tried. They had even tried last night, after arguing, and the effort had ended, quite literally for her, in tears. When they first got together it was not unusual for them to do it three times a day. They did it in cabs, in the kitchen, and once with her leaning out their living room window at night with all the lights on. Ever since the initial argument about their child's potential Jewishness, they did it only before bed, and only in bed, and, as far as she knew, he had not come once. And this was a man who took the greatest and sincerest pleasure in the sight of his own orgasm of anyone she had ever been with. Post-argument, the moment she came he would kiss her, withdraw, and roll over to sleep. The one time she asked him about this he had denied it, and then, she was sure, he began faking his orgasms. Twice now he had made his coming noises, and after he fell asleep she had squatted on the toilet with her hand cupped beneath her, to no avail. Last night he had not been able to get hard at all, which he blamed on the wine, and then the argument, and then the wine. She wondered why they were otherwise getting along so well and had the brief, horrified thought that maybe couples in newly dead marriages got along in a way akin to the cheerfulness of people about to kill themselves.

"Honey?" She was wounded, a little, by his lack of response. "Room service?"

Still writing. "Sure, if you want."

She picked up the phone and listened to the harsh European dial tone, so unlike the organic lushness of the North American dial tone. She thought about what to order and looked over at him again. "What do you suppose is considered a good tip for room service here? Two Celtic crosses or three?"

He did not look up. "I think you use real money for that, sweetie."

She replaced the phone and began to unbutton her shirt. Off came her skirt. Underwear, be gone. Her socks were last. Amazingly, he had not yet noticed, though two-thirds of his back was to her. She swung her legs to the floor and walked softly over to him, careful now to stay out of his peripheral vision, appalled by the sudden determination of her . . . lust? No. She did not even feel particularly wanton. She just needed to know if he still wanted her. She was self-conscious about her stomach, both proud of and slightly concerned by it (she touched it sometimes, when she was alone, as though it were an heirloom of uncertain provenance), and she wondered if this was why he refused to come, if somewhere within him was an animal self that considered her body territory that had already been marked. She was upon her husband now and began rubbing his shoulders. He had a big dog's dumb love of rubs and scratchings and at once his body went slumpy in his chair. His writing fist opened and his pencil toppled over and rolled to the bottom of the page.

"God," he said. "*Really* needed that."

"Stressed out?" She glanced at the page on which he had

been writing and saw her name several times. Unlike him, to turn inward—to focus his writing upon his *wife,* of all people. Maybe the time for the American voice really *was* over. She looked away.

"I don't know. A little."

She knew his eyes were closed. That he made no effort to conceal what he was writing made her less worried.

"That feels *so* nice."

"It's supposed to."

For a while he did not say anything. Then: "While you were asleep"—his voice had changed, become somehow artificially official—"I was reading the guidebook. And I noticed we're not too far away from Rome's biggest synagogue."

She realized that at his mention of "synagogue" she had begun to pincer his deltoid too aggressively.

"So what I thought was that maybe tomorrow we could go there together. I thought maybe you'd like that. I'd like it, too. Maybe seeing it will make me . . ."

"Make you what?" She was no longer rubbing him but was rather behind him, bent over, her hands behind her back, her chin set upon his shoulder, thrillingly conscious of the secret of her nakedness.

"Maybe it will help us." He started to turn around in his chair. "I should warn you that it's a synagogue designed by two Christian archi— Sweetie. You're naked."

"Sit back," she said.

He smiled in a worried way. "What are you doing?"

"Just sit back."

He did, and she went to her knees. She undid his belt with the poised delicacy of someone who already knew what the gift she was unwrapping contained. Without prompting he lifted his ass off the seat, allowing her to tug off his jeans. She was relieved to find that he was already hard. It had been a hot day and he

18

smelled like the skin underneath a not-recent bandage. She did not mind. She did not muck around either. His cock was as warm as a mouthful of blood.

"Jesus," he said, and she felt his whole body flex. She was not a huge fan of performing oral sex and took a fairly workman-like approach to the act. But now she imagined the inside of her mouth as being florally soft and smooth, and was conscious, suddenly, that she would never know what this felt like, disappearing into the mouth of another. The realization made her bizarrely excited. "Jewish girls like to fuck." A Catholic boyfriend of hers had said that to her once. She certainly liked to fuck. But she had corrected the boyfriend: "Reform Jewish girls like to fuck." (Later, after they broke up but stayed friendly, he began dating a black woman and told her, "Black girls like to fuck." She was devastated.) She wondered if her husband did not want to come in her anymore because she was Jewish.

"Jesus," he said again. He was thrusting lightly. Even the most artful blow job grows repetitive, and, as a thought experiment, she imagined getting divorced. She supposed she would have to if he refused to allow their child to be Jewish. But she wondered if she could. She knew the story of his parents' divorce. It was one of the first intimate stories about himself he had ever told her. His mother used to put him in the back seat of her silver Cadillac convertible—a car, he said, as long as a submarine—and drop by Ernie's Party Store (she remembered that name, its small-town perfection) for comic books. On the days she took him to Ernie's she always put the top up. (This was a woman who kept the top down even when it was sprinkling.) While he read his comic books his mother parked out in front of a strange house in a neighborhood not terribly far from their house. Always she made sure to park in the shade, at a discreet diagonal angle from the strange house. She would be gone for only a little while, she would tell him, rolling down his window before leaving him to his crime-fighting mutants and walking hurriedly toward the strange house. On the fifth or sixth time she took him there, he asked whom she was going to see. His mother said she was going to see a friend. After the eighth or ninth time he asked what she had been doing with her friend. She said, *It's a surprise. For Daddy. So please don't tell him.* What kind of surprise? She did not answer, so he was forced to hazard a child's guess: *A surprise party?* He naturally misunderstood her tears in response to this guess: he thought they were tears of happiness. Obviously, he could not stand—no little boy could stand—being the secret sharer of such exciting information for long. When he told his father about the party, asking him to promise he would pretend to be surprised, his father said he would, then asked a few short, expert questions, nodded, and walked from the room. His mother moved out the next day. So it was not surprising that the whole question of divorce was a rather knotty one for him. She wondered if he could divorce her. She had read once that every marriage was between a teacher and a student. She wondered what would have to happen for her to know for certain which one she was. She knew what he thought she was.

And with that, amid the pomp of some magnificent, Sasquatchian sounds, he was coming. She had never let anyone come in her mouth before and was not sure whether to swallow it or what. She was game, but the taste was not at all the seawater harshness she imagined it would be but rather something chemically nondegradable, like pool cleaner. Her mouth dropped open and what must have been half a cup of sperm and drool splatted against the carpet with water-balloon density. He looked down at her, breathing, his eyes crazed.

—

It was a weekday morning, but even so, the night had not been gentle to the streets of Rome. Bits of paper tumbleweeded down the swaybacked sidewalk along the Tiber River, and every twenty yards they came upon a little area that looked as though an ill-disciplined army had bivouacked there: Peroni beer bottles with a single swallow left in them, paper plates made transparent by pizza grease, panino wrappers, even a half-deflated soccer ball. The morning was clear and the sunlight seemed to bronze everything it caught, but the air blew with some strange microscopic grit.

The night had not been gentle with him either. She had actually slept well, but he had awoken her at five a.m. to describe the nightmare he had just experienced. In it he was somehow accepting the best director Academy Award for *Revenge of the Sith,* but no one could hear him speak over the music and then people began laughing at him. When she had told him that she would have laughed, too, were she in the audience, she could hear him sulk in the darkness.

From a distance it did not much resemble a synagogue. It had a square dome, for one. Closer up it did not much resemble a synagogue either. It kind of looked like a bank. But what did she know? The temples of her youth had looked like junior high schools. She disliked the similarity of Christian churches' bland majesty and had never really believed that they were built with love. There was something arctic about their devotion, and the brutal awe she felt inside the churches of Rome annoyed her—a (more or less) innocent opinion, voiced on their first day here, to which her husband had responded with such a grenade of ire that he had apologized almost instantly.

It occurred to her, as they approached, that she did not really care to see Rome's synagogue. The notion that they might discover anything here together struck her as fancifully at odds with what she knew were his real feelings. She was being coddled, mollified. She felt unwell. The only thing worse than going into this synagogue would be *telling* him she did not want to go into this synagogue. Perhaps, in her own way, she was coddling *him*. It was too soon for their marriage, she felt certain, to have this many secret motivations.

Standing before the synagogue, she took in the penitentiary inelegance of its surrounding black gates, its eggshell marble, its colonnaded ledges and tiers, and its small but noticeable number of broken windows. No longer a bank at all, but the mansion of some once-wealthy eccentric who had gone broke in the middle of an ambitious and possibly demented renovation. All around the synagogue was a typical Roman neighborhood of sun-bleached buildings with windows covered with parsley-green wooden shutters. This neighborhood, she had read, had once been predominantly Jewish—it was indeed still called the Jewish Ghetto—but in recent years many of the Jews had been getting priced out. On the corner of the synagogue's block stood a Plexiglas box, inside of which a hatless police officer read a newspaper. As they walked toward what they guessed was the proper entrance, several signs let it be known that the Museo Ebraico di Roma was currently under VIDEO SORVEGLIATA.

She waited at the bottom of a stone staircase while he went up to an unpromising black-tinted glass door. Before he could give the handle an experimental pull a short, bald man, whose near-perfect caricature of squat Semitic brusqueness was offset only by his pink sweater, opened the door and asked, "You pay ticket?" When her husband said no, the man jerked his thumb in a vaguely obscene way toward another gate farther down the block. Here they found a doorbell, which she pressed. She hated doorbells that did not make a corresponding sound for the benefit of the doorbeller and, fearing it was broken, pressed again after fifteen seconds. With a disapproving buzz the gate popped open.

They walked without comment through an open-air yellow corridor, the walls of which were affixed with chunks of old Sicilian synagogues, pieces of alms boxes, ancient fragments of synagogue doorjambs, all of them stamped with Hebrew letters, some of which she thought she might have recognized. All passed through her with no more moment than that of a parachutist through a cloud. He had already gone ahead into the lobby, where apparently tours were booked. The young woman who sat behind the ticket desk with a modest presence informed her that entering the synagogue cost seven euros. "An English tour begins at seven fifteen," she said. "We will call you."

She paid hoping he had not overheard this, but when she gave him his ticket he was smirking.

"It costs seven euros to get in?"

"It's a museum," she said.

"So's Saint Peter's. They don't charge you to go in there because it's still a functional place of worship."

She concentrated on not being angry. "The bone church cost money to get into."

"The bone *crypt* cost money to get into. The church above it was free. And the bone crypt asked for a donation, not seven euros."

She looked at him, nodding. "So you really plan on being a dickhead about this."

He winced in the stalwart way of a man being injected with something intended to benefit him. "Permission to apologize?"

"Authorization to forgive is pending." She poked him in the belly. "Behave and it might come through."

The museum's capsule history of Rome's Jewish community was set out on a series of large, thick, spot-glossed posterboards. While they stood before the first of these highly reflective plaques, dim and faceless ghost versions of themselves stared out as though from an inescapable dimension. She read one subject heading ("From Judaei to Jews: The Jews of Rome during the Middle Ages"), noted a quote from a twelfth-century visitor to Rome ("Two hundred Jews live there, who are very much respected"), and was not surprised by how quickly the story turned unhappy ("The burning of the Talmud in 1553 dealt a terrible blow to the tradition of Talmudic studies in Rome").

"I didn't know that," her husband said, reading a different section.

"What's that?"

"*Get* was the term for the deed of separation between a man and woman, the deed of 'divorcement,' and that this might be where the word *ghetto* comes from."

She refocused. It was uncanny: every paragraph was filled with information vague enough to be uninteresting and precise enough to be soporific. She tried again, engaging in a little contest with herself to see how long she could hang in there: "The Italian *minhag* is also known as *minhag Kahal Italiani*. Its origins are closest to the land of Israel, as are the German and the Romaniote Greek liturgy as well as an ancient French rite that oh my god oh my god boring kill me boring."

She turned to the middle of the room, where a glass display case as high as her belly contained a thick old medieval Pentateuco. A book; it had that going for it at least. Her husband was now across the room, so she joined him in his study of an old map of the city, done in the quaintly incompetent medieval cartographic style. He moved on and she followed him to a piecrust-colored tombstone with a menorah on it. She resented not being

24

able to tell him how bored she was. She was interested in the traditions, she thought, sort of, but not in the objects themselves. How could this be? She wondered if her husband might not in fact have a point. What *were* such traditions without the tent pegs of religious belief keeping them in place?

Soon they were called and met their guide back in the lobby. His name was David, pronounced Da-*veed*. He had short brown hair, the hawkish Roman nose that had no Jewish or Gentilic preference, perfect pink ears, hydraulically sincere eyebrows, small catlike teeth, and a weirdly furrowed brow for someone so young. They joined the ten other English-speaking tourists who had already gathered around David, only two of whom looked American: a blinking, sport-coated father and his exquisitely manqué son, who wore cargo pants and a maroon Roma soccer jersey. They were from one of the overfed states, it looked like.

"Please don't take pictures," David began, "inside or outside. Yarmulkes are provided for the men to cover their heads. Women must cover their shoulders as well." With a smile he handed a shawl to an Asian woman old enough to know that her pink Hello Kitty tank top was 100 percent unacceptable. The men then fished yarmulkes from a basket that David held out to them. Her husband looked at his with a chuckle and plopped it upon his head with good-sport disdain. It looked even sillier on him than she was expecting.

David proceeded to escort his troop downstairs into the building's basement synagogue—a second, smaller Sephardic synagogue—the centerpiece of which was a room so colorful it looked as though a rainbow had exploded in it. They sat in the first two rows of the uncomfortable wooden pews while David stood and waited for the others to find their seats.

"So we begin," David began, "our guided tour about the history of our community, which is unique among all the Jews of the West, including the United States. The Ashkenazi-Sephardic distinction does not entirely apply to our community."

David spoke on, but she looked around, listening with a sonar-like part of her brain, hearing outlines and occasional distinctions, nothing more.

The altar was draped with gold-tasseled bright blue rugs. Another rug with a gold menorah sewn onto its face was hung on the wall directly across from the altar. The thrones were cast of mottled red marble, their seats covered with thin red cushions. She had a vague sense that one of the thrones was where the Talmud was read during worship. No. All wrong. It was not an altar but a bema, and it faced east; it was also where the Torah, *not* the Talmud, was read. The thrones were where the Torah was *kept*. She had to stop herself from smiling. Years of Hebrew school and her husband doubtlessly knew more about Judaic ritual than she did. She tried to figure out which of her fellow tourists were Jewish and which were not, an impulse she would have found unforgivable in anyone but herself.

David was now taking questions. "Jews lived in the ghetto for three hundred years," he told the Asian woman. "We Italian Jews also became the only Jewish community to be put back in a ghetto *after* being emancipated in 1798. We had to remain there until 1860, and this was long after almost all other members of European Jewry had been granted full legal rights. Florentine Jews suffered the same fate, earning their emancipation in 1808 but being returned to the ghetto in 1815."

Someone then asked about a gated area behind the pews. "That," David said, "is where women sit." Several hands instantly shot up. David laughed and, without calling on anyone, explained the religious reasons for this. That was when she noticed her husband slip off his yarmulke and search around his immediate area with the finicky distaste of someone working out where to stash a plug of chewed gum. He finally gave up and orphaned his yarmulke on the empty seat next to him.

She elbowed him. "Come on," she whispered. "Put it back on."

He whispered back: "Fuck that. They segregate the sexes? Fuck. That."

"I'm glad," she said, still whispering, "that you've found something to be angry about. But this is an Orthodox synagogue."

"I can't be angry?" He was no longer whispering.

"No, you can. What you're not allowed to be is surprised."

As they were leaving, the stout American father took a picture. David rushed over to him with frantically, though still politely, waving hands. "No photos, please. For security purposes."

The man said, "I'm just taking one of the rug here."

David smiled in what she recognized as tourist-honed, yeah-it-*is*-crazy ingratiation. "Our synagogue was once attacked, by terrorists, and so security is important to us. Please understand."

The man's mouth opened. "When was the synagogue attacked?"

"In 1982."

Her husband burst out laughing.

"Security is important to us," David said to the man in a loud, dislocated voice she knew was directed at her husband. "Upstairs in the Orthodox synagogue you can see for yourself our broken windows. Those were shattered in the attack, and we have never repaired them to remind us of what happened here."

"Was it Muslims?" the man wanted to know.

David smiled. "Let's go upstairs to the Orthodox synagogue."

The trip took them briefly outside. Their feet made wet splashing noises on the gravel walkway that led to the Orthodox synagogue's wooden doors, which David held open for everyone, nodding in identical welcome at each person as he or she passed. Inside were dozens of rows of wooden pews, the baker's-chocolate-colored joinery of which was truly lovely. David allowed them all a few moments to explore. She saw that many individual seats were affixed with little gold plaques bearing the names of the worshippers for whom they were reserved. She then noted that the entirety of the synagogue's first row was labeled EX DEPORTATO. She did not need any Italian to know who sat there and why. She looked up into the square dome, filled with a sparkling airborne cathedral of sunlight. And there they were—the synagogue's broken windows, through which shoots of bamboo-colored light beamed.

David began his tour. The synagogue was inaugurated in 1904. The columns were hewn from some rare marble, the name of which she neglected to catch. From the black candelabras and chandeliers to the boiled-milk marble, you could see that the synagogue's Christian architects had worked in what was called the Syrio-Babylonian style.

"And where do the women sit?" one of the other tourists asked—a small, bespectacled woman with a round face. She looked the woman over: yellow smoker's fingers, trembling hamster nose, an intense grudge-seeking manner about her.

"Women," David answered, "can sit upstairs, behind the gate, if there's room."

"If there's room," her husband echoed loud enough for David to hear.

David looked at him and was about to answer when he noticed that her husband was no longer wearing his yarmulke. That their exchange would now be one of regulation rather than confrontation seemed to relax David. "Excuse me, sir—there are yarmulkes in back." He moved on to answer another question, but her husband did not move. She felt her face grow warm as the rest of her body chilled like a licked finger raised into the wind. David looked back to her husband a minute later and, still smiling, said, "Sir, please help yourself to a yarmulke in back."

She said her husband's name and gently pushed him rearward, toward the yarmulke basket. Her hands were on his chest and she realized he had never buttoned up his shirt. He still refused to move; she felt as though she were pushing one of the synagogue's thick marble columns.

They now had the full interest of the tour group. With a kind of herd-animal practicality, she found herself stepping away from her husband. She had felt their eyes picking holes in him, in her, in *them*. Remarkable: after putting only a few feet of separation between her and her husband, no one was looking at her anymore. She was ashamed by her relief.

"Sir," David said again. There was no need to say anything else.

Watching her husband prepare for an argument was similar to watching a boxer throw off his robe. She knew what was coming but was still not fully prepared for the brazen impudence of what he said or the sneering pride with which he said it: "So I'm not going to wear a yarmulke."

David blinked. She wondered if anything like this had happened to him before.

"Sir, you must cover your head."

Her husband answered in the same cruel voice he had used two nights ago to disparage her book. "And what's going to happen to me if I don't?"

She had the sense of watching someone fall down a flight of stairs in slow motion and noting the various stages of injury.

David was no longer smiling. "You will have to leave." His voice was tight; each word had a small, cold exactness.

One member of the group, an Englishman no older than twenty-five who was wearing a red Che Guevara T-shirt, said, "*Christ,* mate—cover your fuckin' head."

"Why should he?" This was the short, yellow-fingered woman.

"Out of respect," the young Englishman said.

It was to this young prole that her husband now turned. "I would happily cover my head if this synagogue allowed women to sit with men. It doesn't. I don't respect that or the god our friend David here thinks tells him this is right, so why *should* I cover my head?"

Her hand leapt up and landed with an open-palmed smack against her forehead. She said his name again, and again.

"Sir," David said. "This is our place of worship and community. You are here as our guest. If you don't cover your head, I will have to ask you to leave."

Her husband grinned as though this were exactly the argument he had been waiting for David to mount. "You charged me seven euros to come into your place of worship, so I think you kind of lose the right to tell me what I can or cannot wear while I'm in here."

"How does *that* work?" This was the American father in the sport coat. The man's son, she saw, was laughing.

David sighed and withdrew from his pocket a cellular phone. He speed-dialed, spoke a few words in Italian, then snapped shut the phone—a harsh, guillotine sound. He contemplated her husband now as though from a great height. "You will be escorted from this synagogue if you refuse to cover your head."

Her husband's smile was a fragment from some former, exploded confidence. "You're throwing me out of the synagogue."

David nodded. "You will be escorted from this synagogue if you—"

"Get rid of this douche bag!" The boy who a moment ago had been laughing said this. In fact, he was still laughing, which made her husband's stand seem, at that moment, even more ludicrous. "Dude, like what is wrong with you?"

Her husband said nothing while his eyes wandered from one member of their group to another. He avoided her and David, which she hopefully took as an indication that he was about to apologize. Instead he told the group, with great gravity, "Social justice isn't just about hating George Bush, you know."

The bald man in the pink sweater emerged from a room adjacent to the bema and began to walk toward her husband. At this her husband turned to her in something close to lip-licking panic. Not that he was being forcefully removed from a place of worship—she knew he would tell this story, with certain redactions, for years—but rather at the thought of everything else that had been set into motion here.

The man in the pink sweater was upon him. His lips were wet in a way that made her wonder if his breakfast had just been interrupted. The man looked at her husband, then at her, and then back at her husband. "We leave now," he said, relying, for the moment, on his presence as reason enough to leave.

Her husband refused to look at the man. Instead he shook his head and muttered, "I paid my seven euros. I'm seeing the synagogue. Not leaving."

The man in the pink sweater, who seemed both covetous of and frightened by the opportunity to use force, was then summoned by David. They spoke in fast hushed spirals of Italian. David's opinion, whatever that might be, seemed to win the day. The man in the pink sweater shook his head while David made another phone call. Soon enough, the hatless police officer from the corner cubicle outside entered the synagogue—and, oddly, crossed himself.

At the sound of the door opening, her husband turned. At the sight of the approaching expressionless officer, he sighed. "Come on," he said to her. His tone was light; she could nearly hear his mind rearranging what had just happened into nothing more than an amusing misunderstanding. "Let's get thrown out of the synagogue together at least."

He stuck out his hand: his old trick. She took the hand and walked with him past the officer. As the box of daylight at the end of the synagogue aisle grew larger and brighter, she was surprised by how quiet it was—and she knew this, this sound, this sound of hope collapsing, of separate divinities forming, of exclusion, of closed doors, of one story's end.

My Interview with
the Avenger

ESQUIRE / "THE HEROES ISSUE" / JANUARY 2007

Celebrated, suspected, and sometimes hated (not to mention very, very famous), the Avenger at long last steps from the crime-fighting shadows—and gets far more from our reporter than he bargained for.

by Tim Jonah

This is a story about heroes. Yes, it's also a profile of a famous man—a "celebrity," for lack of a less hideous word—but it's first and foremost a story about heroes and what they mean. Of course, nearly everyone remembers how and when the man now known as the Avenger first made his existence public. Most origin stories are cumbrous with mythic overlay, but the Avenger arrived in twinkly, almost pointillistic detail. There was nothing to add to the story to make it better; it defeated augmentation.

New York City, 2003. Remember? A night in late January. A pair of muggers approach two Japanese tourists unwise enough to have wandered deep into the swards of Central Park at too late an hour. Moments after the muggers assault the tourists, who don't resist them, a fifth party rushes into the fray. "We don't know what happened," one of the tourists tells the police afterward. "It happened so fast." One of the muggers, speaking to the police later that night from his bed at New York

Presbyterian—his colleague's broken jaw ruled out any corroborating statement—is more descriptive: "He came out of nowhere, sprayed us with some shit, hit us a bunch of times, and cuffed us to each other. Then he was gone." The *Post*'s headline: "HE CAME OUT OF NOWHERE": GOOD SAMARITAN FOILS PARK THUGS. The *Times* strikes a less populist, more skeptical note: NYPD GRATEFUL FOR, CONCERNED BY ACTIONS OF PARK VIGILANTE. No follow-up; no one comes forward. Just one of those weird New York stories of a person stepping from the everythingness of the city before retreating anonymously back into it.

Then, weeks later, and once again in Central Park, a purse-snatching teenager from the Bronx is chased down shortly before midnight by a man he later describes as "the fastest white dude ever." The man, wearing a black ski mask and utility belt, extracts the purse with minimal force. He also extends some friendly advice that will, of course, later become legendary: "If you really do plan to continue in this line of work, I'd advise more cardio." The next evening the victim receives her purse, by courier, at her Upper West Side home. The sender of the purse lists a nonexistent Manhattan post office box under an equally nonexistent name, but he does include a typed note: "I believe you lost this last night." The note is signed in all caps ("THE AVENGER"), but this small pertinence does not fully register for weeks.

The Avenger has been with us now for almost four years—long enough that those first months when no one was sure what to call him can be recalled only through the same murky vale as a pre-9/11 skyline. The "Central Park Vigilante" was the NYPD's preferred agnomen. The *Times* opted for "New York City's Anonymous Self-Appointed Guardian" but sometimes, and grudgingly, resorted to "the so-called Avenger."

In the beginning, though, he is for most of us not a person

but a question: *Did you hear about that guy?* Because, by that point, everyone had. Shortly after the purse snatcher (who was never charged) had come forward to the press, and immediately after the purse's owner had been photographed smiling while holding up her mysterious note for the cover of the *Times*'s city section, two burglars are found beaten and hog-tied on the floor of a Chelsea brownstone. Their situation is brought to the police's attention by an anonymous pay phone 911 call believed to have been made by That Guy himself. The *Post*'s headline, in letters half a foot high, tells us all we need to know: HE'S BACK! Our news cycles would have a different algorithm now, synced to the actions of a man no one could find and whose actions no one could predict.

One thing was clear: New York City had an entirely new kind of inhabitant. Was he a less vengeful version of Bernhard Goetz? A witty sociopath? A professional headline seeker? A nut? A saint? *Who was he?* More than that: *Why was he?* Years later, no one is any closer to answering either question.

Fourteen months ago I wrote an essay for this magazine ("The Avenger Dies for Our Sins," September 2005) about why I believed the Avenger's actions were, from a legal and civic point of view, dangerous. I had not, of course, interviewed the Avenger for my essay. He has given only one interview, by phone, to Larry King. This was shortly after coming to terms with the New York City Police Department and being granted, in absentia, by Mayor Michael Bloomberg the dubious and unprecedented legal status as "an honorary constabulary deputy of the greatest city on earth." The Avenger tried to explain to King what, legally, this meant, but even he was not sure. The interview, at one point the third-most-watched clip in YouTube history, is famously unhinged: the man we imagined as our incorruptible guardian sounded more like a tranqed-out crackpot. (Only later did we learn that the Avenger was nursing a concussion after falling off a fire escape, as he explained in the second of the three letters he has sent to the *Times*.) But because he was finally being allowed to continue his mission without any interference from the authorities—though he must, at all times, report his planned whereabouts—the Avenger had finally elected to speak directly to the people. And despite his evasions ("I am not able at this time to tell you why I'm doing this") and chilly bravado ("I am a most unique man"), we responded. We wanted him. We *needed* him.

We also hounded him, occasionally tried to capture him ourselves, and pointed an unending series of fingers at those we believed *were* him. This is why I wrote my article. This is why I believed the Avenger was doing more harm than good. Hardly any of the criminals he's stopped, and often beaten, have been convicted. There was, and remains, no legal precedent for what the Avenger is doing. By working in secrecy, by rejecting the elaborate and, yes, sometimes frustrating evidential byways upon which American jurisprudence has settled, the Avenger, I wrote, was a *negation* of American justice, not its embodiment. Viewed bloodlessly and unsentimentally, he was probably a criminal himself.

The thing about my essay was I knew I was right and I knew I was wrong. I was right because all the Avenger had done was reify the same tired old vigilante fantasy that exists in make-believe's less exalted basements—that is, in comic books and video games. I was wrong because the Avenger changed things in ways no one could have predicted. He did not rise up from a time of untrammeled chaos, and he was certainly not the vox of any populi. He was, instead, the first person in our national public life in a very long time to suggest that virtue and not fame could come first, that virtue could exist and not be exploited by fame. As time went on, as he evaded capture, and as he refused to disclose his identity, it became clear that the Avenger really did not want the attention—at least, not per se. He actually believed in what he was doing. And he always (as I conceded in my article) seemed paranormally aware of exactly how much damage to deal out to those whose crimes he stopped. In fact, he didn't even seem all that vindictive. Many of the roughly seventy criminals he has disarmed, coldcocked, limb-snapped, and leg-swept today profess admiration for him, with a few even crediting the Avenger with the back they have shown their former lives of crime. Yes, some have sued, but this has gone nowhere. The Avenger was paradigm-shiftingly new, and it turns out it's impossible to be entirely wrong or entirely right about something we don't yet have the vocabulary to describe.

Days after my article appeared on newsstands, I received a letter from the Avenger. It had been postmarked in New York City. Strangely, and somewhat menacingly, it was addressed to my unlisted home address. The return address was that of this magazine, with a simply typed "A." above it. My article had obviously riled and angered him, as part of me certainly hoped it would. The Avenger's tone was curt, and I've agreed not to quote his letter here, but he invited me, at a time and place of his choosing, to meet. I heard nothing else for weeks. Then he wrote again. I was to journey by train outside the city to the Goldens Bridge stop, wait forty-five minutes, and then follow precisely detailed directions into the nearby woodlands. I was to come alone—and he would know if I was being followed. I believed this. The man had evaded one of the biggest manhunts in New York City history for almost two years. Since his honorary constabulary deputization, I'd felt very alone in my opposition to the Avenger. I told no one but my editor of my plans to meet him. My editor asked, only half jokingly, if I planned on bringing a weapon. I had not even considered this until my editor mentioned it. I then wished he hadn't.

Forty-five minutes, when you're waiting to meet the Avenger, is a long time, and while standing on the train platform at Goldens Bridge, I thought about all the reading I'd done about his peculiar species of costumed vigilantism. Others before the Avenger have taken to the streets, of course. There is Terrifica, a self-styled Valkyrie who patrols New York City bars to prevent predatory men from taking advantage of drunken women; Captain Jackson of Jackson, Michigan, "an officially sanctioned independent crime fighter" whose group, the Crimefighter Corps, works Jackson's troublous streets to little or no effect; Mr. Silent of Indianapolis; Ferox of Salt Lake City; Polar Man of the Canadian Arctic. There are more. A website called the World Superhero Registry exists to keep track of these people. Look it up and marvel at human aspiration at its most quietly noble and utterly deranged. One thing you'll note is that the Avenger isn't found on this site. Many of the registered superheroes I contacted for comment on the Avenger refused to say a word on the record about him. Off the record, the dissertations began. He's a glory hound. A menace. They work *with* the system, you'll hear. The Avenger is out for himself.

The men and women listed on the World Superhero Registry are without exception grassroots, niche-based operators whose Lycra often poorly contains their girth. They are, in effect, noble clowns. But a few have tried to follow the Avenger's more dangerous, socially outlying path, the results of which have been either vaguely comic or utterly tragic. In Los Angeles a hopeful who strapped two Tasers to his wrists and went by the imaginative name of Taserman accidentally zapped himself during his unsuccessful prevention of a carjacking. The Boomerang Kid was shot by unimpressed gangsters in Las Vegas. Miami's Sunstroke was arrested for assault after being heckled. Chicago's Wolfreign was nicked for solicitation. These are (and, in the Boomerang Kid's case, were) not people like you or me, and further investigation into each of these "heroes" revealed long histories of psychiatric inpatient care. But they weren't much like the man they were attempting to imitate either.

While the Avenger has no superpowers, he's thought to be a fine and possibly gifted martial artist. His bravery and physical strength are also well established. The existence of his utility belt has been confirmed, along with its assortment of nonlethal instruments: pellets of tear gas, smoke bombs, a supply of plastic zip ties. At least a dozen of his prey have reported catching eyefuls of Mace before being beaten. The claim by one criminal to have shot the Avenger in the chest seems to validate rumors of a specially thin Kevlar vest.

Even after all this time and all that's been written about him, I thought on the Goldens Bridge platform, *there's still so much we don't know.* Of no other comparably famous person could this be said—and I've spent a good portion of my career writing about, and contemplating, the famous. I looked off into the bran-colored brush thicket and up a hilly copse of leafless trees in which I knew he waited. My watch's alarm sounded. I'd set it because I wanted to be exact, as exact as the man I was about to meet. The longest and shortest forty-five minutes of my life were up. I headed off to meet the Avenger.

I don't have to go far—perhaps a ten-minute walk from the platform. The Avenger was sitting in a lotus position on a thronelike rock halfway up a hill. The sky, fittingly, had turned dark, and the wind shook the stripped trees around us as though in indistinct warning. But there he was. I lifted my hand in greeting.

Now, there's a question people ask when they learn you've met the Avenger. It's not about what he was wearing (for the record: a black ski mask and plain black hoodless sweatshirt; loose black cargo pants with many marsupial pouches; black Adidas running shoes; a belt, also black, but smaller and more proletarian than I'd imagined and bulging with snap-shut pockets and holsters and plastic protuberances), and it's not what his in-person voice sounds like (confident, accentless, not quite fully grown, all its vitality at the edges rather than the center), and it's not whether he's friendly (read on). The question they ask is: Is he funny?

Because that's the rap on the Avenger, the attribute earned by all those suspiciously rehearsed comments he's made over the years to the people he's both walloped and rescued. The answer is yeah, he's funny. In fact, the very first thing the Avenger said to me, while certainly not hilarious, was funny—or at least mordantly engaging:

"Tell me. Exactly which of your sins do I have to die for?"

I was still walking toward him, hummingbird-hearted. His voice so startled me I momentarily forgot the title of my own anti-Avenger essay. I stopped. "I'm sorry?"

With a grand little flourish he extended his hand. Given the darkness of his garb, his hand's flesh was so contrastingly white it seemed to glow. His only other bits of visible flesh were the twinned circles held within the eyelets of his ski mask and the oblong rectangular cutout around his mouth. His free hand, which remained on his knee, was gloved. " 'The Avenger Dies for Our Sins.' The reason I'm sitting here and the reason you're looking at me."

Now we really *were* looking at each other. "That was my editor's title," I told him. "Pretty sure he meant it as a metaphor."

The Avenger nodded. His eyes, if I had to guess, were brown. "Metaphor? Okay. But kind of a shitty one, in my opinion."

"You have an interest in metaphor?" A stupid thing to say. I knew it even then.

He sat there and said nothing. I'd already disappointed him.

"How," I asked, "do you know no one's going to walk along this path?"

Instantly he held up a device that looked like a cell phone. "I've placed a tiny wire across the trail fifty yards behind me. If someone trips it, this'll vibrate. I can see behind you for another fifty yards. Don't worry. If anyone happens along, I'll be out of sight in thirty seconds, give or take. And you won't be able to follow me, even if you try."

I motioned around at the forest, a thinly treed suburban wild any decent runner could easily navigate. "What about the rest of these woods?"

"I'll take my chances. People tend to stick to paths. It's one of the things that makes criminals so easy to anticipate. Most of us operate along a quantitatively smaller spectrum of choice than we realize."

"But not you."

"If I weren't victim to the same coded inhibitions I wouldn't be very good at predicting the behavior of others, would I? No, I'm the same. The only difference is that I'm aware that when most people appear to have five or six choices, they really only have two." His chin lifted. "If that."

I pulled out my notepad, held it up to him, and asked, "May I?"

A small, annoyed shrug. "Feel free." Two words into my first question, though, he interrupted me: "Why don't you write short stories anymore?"

At this I could do little but laugh. I'd published a book of short stories more than a decade ago. It received a small amount of acclaim and then quickly withdrew from the world of print. The praise was enough to attract a few editors' interest. Within months of the book's publication I began writing magazine journalism, which seemed to provide my talent a less frustrating outlet and my temperament a quicker, more active engagement. "You read my stories," I said. A few reluctant raindrops fell from the sky and pattered onto the autumnally crunchy leaves all around us.

"I've read everything you've written. Everything I could find, at least. I'm nothing if not thorough."

I couldn't say I was surprised. Not really. I'd come here expecting to be outwitted at every turn, but perhaps not so soon—or so intimately. I attempted a graceless flanking move. "Very interesting, Avenger. Why that name, by the way? Is it some reference to the Avengers?"

"I'm not a child. I don't read comic books. Don't ask stupid questions."

This made me angry. "Okay. And I can leave. I didn't come here to be insulted."

The Avenger remained as still as an idol, waiting for me to make good on my threat. Knowing I wouldn't. Then: "I'll be honest, Tim. I didn't care much for your fiction, but the story about the young guy whose brother was killed—that one I enjoyed a lot. And of course your real-life brother was killed, too. Now, what's interesting to me, as a reader, is that you never wrote anything else about your brother's death, even though that story's the best thing you've written. Wouldn't you say? I bet you would. And then what do you do after writing this story? You spend a decade cranking out profiles of Michael Stipe and Will Ferrell."

I looked away. When I was nineteen and he was twenty-five, my brother was shot and killed while trying to intervene in a mugging in Washington, D.C. His killer was never found. "I've written plenty of things besides profiles."

"I've seen your occasional attempts at cultural criticism, yeah. And sometimes you write about violent crime. A fascination of yours, clearly. But—and this is what I, personally, find amazing—you somehow never manage to disclose that your own brother died at the hands of a violent criminal."

My head swung back quickly to face him. "I've written about my brother." And I had. I'd written about my brother for this magazine, five years ago—a long essay about families who'd lost a member to unsolved murder and how, in virtually every case, those families had never recovered; the four horsemen of divorce, substance abuse, depression, and suicide stalked them from the day of the murder on, plucking away the remaining members one by one. Writing that piece proved so harrowing I haven't attempted long-form investigative journalism since.

"You mentioned your brother in two paragraphs in that essay. The only time you've ever truly faced up to what happened is in your short story. Everything else is peripheral."

"I haven't read the story in years. I barely even remember it." Insofar as something could be both true and false, this was it.

The Avenger unfolded his legs and slid off his throne. But he took no further step. "I'm no writer, but if *I'd* suffered what you and your family suffered, and if *I* were writing critically about so-called vigilantism, I might let the reader know what, exactly, was informing my criticism."

"I had more stuff in there about him, at an early point. But I took it out."

The Avenger's head tilted. "And why did you do that?"

"I don't want to exploit my brother."

"You write about celebrities. You might as well exploit your brother."

I put my notebook back into my pocket. Curiously, it had not rained any more than those first few drops. "You asked me here. I didn't ask you. You asked me."

"What did you do after your brother died?"

"How do you dispense Mace? There've been reports you squirt it from a device hidden somewhere on your wrist."

He extended his left arm. What began at his wrist as a jet of liquid became, two feet from its launching point, a fine mist. Within seconds the wind had blown the lightly Tabascoed air my way. My eyes filled with tears.

"Hey," he said. "You asked."

I nodded and rubbed my eyes. "Fair enough. How about the Kevlar vest?"

He lifted up his sweatshirt to reveal a tight black vest that appeared as shiny, and roughly as bullet stopping, as neoprene. "It doesn't look like much, but this'll stop a knife and most small-caliber bullets. A shotgun if I'm far enough away. I've been tapped a few times. One asshole shot me and broke two ribs. People assume I'm indestructible, but I get hurt all the time. More than half of my teeth have been knocked out." His demonstrative smile, which revealed a full set of enviably white choppers, lasted no more than a second. "Mostly dentures. All part of the reason I'm not able to patrol as aggressively or regularly as I'd like. You know, the press amuses me. They write all the time about what I'm planning and even print up little city maps that're supposed to show my patterns. There are no patterns. What they call 'planning' is usually me holding an ice pack to my head, pulling the stitches out of my arm, and taking a splint off my big toe."

"Your vest—you design that yourself?"

He shook his head. "Uh, no. I ordered it from a Dutch company that provides armor for security guards, Halliburton, journalists who work in war zones. It wasn't cheap."

"And how do you make your money?"

"I've invested wisely. It's not like the stuff I use costs all that much. You'd be surprised by what you can get, no questions asked, through mail order. Becoming the Avenger required a financial investment of no more than six or seven thousand dollars. Total."

"And do you—"

"My turn." He crossed his arms. "What did you do after your brother died?"

I thought about how to respond. I'd been in loving relationships where it had taken me many months to talk about my brother, and yet this stranger was asking me to winch up buckets sloshing with emotions and memories for no other apparent reason than his amusement. But I also knew my answer would determine how close to him the Avenger would allow me to get.

"I did a lot of things. Crying was a big one, at first. Cried a lot. Studied aikido for a while. Traveled. Finally I wrote. He was a writer, too, by the way. At least he wanted to be. You don't know that because I've never mentioned it. Not in print, anyway."

"Aikido. That's in one of the stories, too."

"I was fairly serious about it. Then it just seemed stupid. I was never very good. I don't even like to fight."

"Then why—"

"I didn't like feeling weak. I wondered if that's what got my brother killed: his weakness. He had such a good heart, but he was physically weak. That's one of the reasons I wrote my essay about you. I worried you'd inspire people to step into situations they have no business stepping into."

"I'm guessing that was one of the parts you cut out. Too bad. I would have liked that version more, I think."

"Everything I wrote is, from a legal point of view, inarguable."

The Avenger walked toward me. When I almost fell over backpedaling he stopped. "You drew back. Tell me why."

"Because I was afraid. I *am* afraid."

"Afraid of what?"

"Of you."

"What do you think criminals are, now, when I show up?"

"They're afraid."

"Of course they are. Criminals are weak. That's why they're criminals. The criminal impulse *is* weakness—abject, encircling weakness. The police don't understand this. A few academics who study crime actually do get it, but who cares? They're academics. So the question is: How do you oppose criminals? And the answer: By changing their positioning. Most people, like your brother, can't do this. Almost anyone who stands up to a criminal will get hurt. It's the first thing they tell you: Just give 'em your wallet, hand it over. I'd tell you that if you were being mugged, and you look, you know, fairly fit, at least for a writer. Still, hand it over—because that's where *I* come in. I'm the agent of repositioning. That's my work, and I'm the only one who can do it. Most people drawn to what I do are sadists, revenge addicts, morons, or insane. Like the Boomerang Kid or any of those other idiots."

"Do you feel responsible for those people?"

"Not in the least."

I shook my head. "You are a most unique man."

"I was concussed when I said that."

"But you don't dispute it."

"I wish I were more unique. There are any number of crimes

in this city, in this country, that I can't do a thing about. And so I essentially terrorize poor kids who had shitty situations to begin with. Am I happy about that? I am not."

"That was the point I tried to make in my essay."

"I agree with you. And I disagree. Because you have to start somewhere."

"Why are you telling me this? Why not just write another letter to the *Times*?"

For the first and only time that afternoon, the Avenger laughed. "What do you want me to say? 'I am but a shadowy reflection of you. It would take only a nudge to make you like me, to push you out of the light'? I have nothing like that to say. And I have no story to tell you. I asked you here for one reason." He then looked down at his vibro-box. "Which will have to wait, because someone's coming."

With a quickness all the more startling for how completely it surpassed my expectation—oh yes, he *was* fast—the Avenger broke away and ran into the woods, changing direction by wrapping a hooked arm around a birch tree, the momentum of which launched him over a rotten log. He did not look back. And I have not heard from him again. Apparently, he's been inactive since I saw him, which, at the time of this writing, ranks among his longest, most enigmatic silences. Sometimes I allow myself to believe he will finally finish what he had to say that day.

I was still standing in the middle of the path when the couple that had tripped the Avenger's wire came upon me. An older man and woman, arm in arm, plump with retirement, looking at me with cool, New Englandy eyes.

The wary, artificial nature of their silence moved me to say, in a bright, friendly voice, "Hello there!" In other words: *Don't be afraid of the weirdly cheerful maniac in the woods.* Of course, they *were* afraid. By trying to tell them they had nothing to fear I'd only made their fear worse. Do I blame them? Not really. I could have done something terrible, like killing them both, or something even worse, like leaving one of them alive and alone, left to wonder forever why no one was there to stop me.

Punishment

I'm here." This is Steve, calling from Newark. Over squawky airport tumult, Mark supplies Steve with directions, estimates cab fare to midtown, thinks of an acceptable tip, factors in Steve's cheapness, and tacks on an extra five dollars. After hanging up Mark stares at his screensaver's floating spheroid. When he nudges the mouse, his *New York Times* homepage materializes like a nightmare: Serb forces are attacking Kosovo rebels, the Unabomber has pleaded guilty, and look, more revelations of Monica and Bill. (Speaking of which: Jesus fucking *Christ,* Mr. President.) Mark abandons his desk, steps across the hallway, and without knocking leans against the jamb of William Stanley Jerome's office.

Jerome is behind his desk, hunched over—a caricature of concentration—reading a manuscript.

"I'm leaving early today," Mark says. "If you want me to write those captions for the Whitman piece you better pick the photos you wanna use now."

Jerome's prematurely baggy face lifts. His glasses, as tiny as a gemologist's, give him a misleadingly doddering air. He has that bowling-pin build that allows overweight men to appear thin while seated. The top button of his rumpled white shirt is undone, below which a tug-loosened yellow tie hangs with sad indifference. Somewhere down the hall a phone chirps. Beneath the sound are the horn-spiked tides of midtown Manhattan, twelve stories below. With a pained squint Jerome returns to the manuscript. "Forget the Whitman piece. It's postponed. Did we talk about your leaving early?"

"We did."

Jerome gestures toward the empty chair in front of his desk. "Sit. You're making me nervous."

His office is large and tidy, a small bonsai tree on the sill lending the space a methodical Japanese spareness. The one hint of disorder is found on the slightly bowed planks of his bookcase, the volumes of which obey no known schema of alphabetics or category but are instead shelved according to a mysterious system in some way related to how Jerome came to possess them.

After a few moments Jerome stops reading and planes the manuscript's loose pages against his desktop. When finished he holds it across his desk with the flair of issuing a summons. "You want?"

Mark takes the manuscript. "Sure. What is it?"

"I ask for five thousand words on a Conrad biography, I get a C-minus book report of *Nostromo*. See if you can't make something of it this weekend."

William Stanley Jerome is the editor of a prestigious, respectfully unread tabloid-sized book review that has been kept at a manageable loss for a decade now by the benefaction of a bookish widow from Riverdale. Mark has been there a little shy of a year. His official title is Assistant to William Stanley Jerome, Editor-in-Chief, a formulation that seemed, at first blush, rather grandiose. Upon taking the job, Mark was briefed on Jerome's tendency to dismiss assistants for crimes such as leaving the umlaut off Günter Grass in interoffice memos. Never before has Jerome entrusted Mark to "make something" of a piece he himself has commissioned. Mark sits there in appreciative silence, staring at the orphaned pages.

Jerome leans back in his chair. "What is it? You've got that sullen, misunderstood look of yours."

Mark sets the pages aside, heeding the implicit *at ease* by throwing one blue-jeaned leg over the other. "A friend of mine's in town for the weekend. With his girlfriend. That's actually why I'm leaving early."

Jerome attempts to find, among his endless mental microfiche, a transcript of some prior conversation. The blunt, nicotine-dyed fingers of Jerome's free hand beckon. "A chemist, your friend. Steve. From . . . Dallas?"

"Chemical engineer. From Houston. Close, though." And Mark stares inertly at the faint brown diamond pattern on Jerome's yellow tie.

The Punishers. When Mark and Steve were boys in Upper Michigan, that's what they called themselves. Together they formed Holy Family Catholic School's two-man junta. Come August, as their classmates shopped for spiral notebooks and book bags, Steve selected an unsuspecting handful for terrorization, typically picking out mouthy weaklings and conscientious objectors to contact sport. Their punishings were quick and merciless, as unexplained as they were premeditated, issued within the tiled echo chamber of school bathrooms or along the wooded footpath that shortcutted to their town's flushest subdivision. Only when their victims had curled into humiliated fetal positions and sworn themselves to silence did Mark and Steve yield.

He and Steve were unlikely bullies. In any adult proximity they became as polite as census takers. They were excellent students and had been anointed with boyish good looks that, at least for Steve, would later become handsomeness. Near the beginning of their eighth-grade year, Steve's father was hired away to

Indiana. After Steve left, Mark felt as though he'd emerged from a trance. During his junior year of high school, he racked up the highest SAT score in the history of Flat Rock, Michigan. At Yale, while reading for an introductory philosophy class, Mark first happened upon Arendt's "banality of evil." Instantly he snapped shut his book and, even though they rarely spoke anymore, rang up Steve in Pasadena, where he attended Caltech as an engineering major, a field Mark dismissed, then and now, as mathematics for people who hated ideas. "Do you remember all that Punisher stuff from when we were kids?" Mark had asked him.

"Yeah," Steve said.

"Why do you suppose we did that?"

The cadence of Steve's silence was indistinguishable from the line's transcontinental hum. "I don't know," Steve finally said. "Who cares?"

But no. Mark tells Jerome none of this. Instead he opts for a thumbnail of misspent youth: "When Steve and I were in grade school together we used to get in trouble. Pick on other kids. Bully them, really. We were . . . we were pretty bad."

Jerome says nothing for a moment. Then, arms crossed: "Not only a promising editor, but an erstwhile hoodlum."

Within Mark, the antlers of guilt and exhilaration lock. The first time Jerome has said anything to him that might be reasonably mistaken for a compliment. "We've seen each other half a dozen times since we were twelve," Mark says. "I don't think he's even coming here to see me. I'm more like a convenient excuse to visit New York for the first time." Mark is just trying to make conversation and say interesting things, but then realizes: *Wait. That's actually probably true, isn't it?* This realization settles in his stomach with a bleak weight.

Jerome spins portside in his swivel chair and flips up a single blind. "You've read Nietzsche?"

"In translation."

" 'The evil who are happy' "—Jerome lets the blind snap shut—" 'a species the moralists bury in silence.' "

"For the record, I never said Steve was happy. Or, you know, evil."

Jerome is smiling now. " 'When we have to change our mind about a person, we hold the inconvenience he causes us very much against him.' "

"Nietzsche again?"

Jerome sighs like a teacher glimpsing, much too late, the limitations of his best student.

A call. "Mr. Mileskoo here to see you," Lunice, the review's Haitian secretary, tells Mark from the lobby an hour later. Before Lunice terminates the interoffice connection Mark hears Steve correct her attempt to pronounce *Mileski*.

Mark last saw Steve during Christmas break two years ago in a crowded Flat Rock bar. They embraced awkwardly, like a couple long divorced; Steve explained his presence with the unrevealing cliché of "passing through." Emblazoned on Steve's sweatshirt were the Greek letters of a Caltech fraternity. They spoke for four minutes, long enough for Steve to assail the East Coast, the Ivy League, Yale, Yale's football team, the liberal arts in general, and English majors in particular. *Never again,* Mark thought, smiling, as their conversation stalled and Steve turned to chat up someone else. *I will never see you again*. He recalled this pledge only three weeks ago, after he'd haltingly agreed to Steve's cold-call suggestion that he and his new girlfriend, Danielle, "pop out" for the weekend.

Mark opens the lobby door to find Steve seated, a large, sturdy black suitcase at his feet. In Steve's hands is not one of the complimentary copies of the review stacked on the table next to him but *Muscle & Fitness*.

Steve stuffs the magazine into his suitcase's side pocket and, in one smooth motion, stands. Mark's erstwhile best friend is necklessly beyond the point where fitness becomes grotesque. Never tall to begin with, Steve now resembles a short tan comic-book mesomorph. He is wearing a tight white short-sleeved dress shirt with a floppy cotton collar and tight pressed slacks the color of sandstone. Steve strides toward Mark and shakes his hand as though simultaneously attempting to crush his phalanges and dislocate his shoulder. "Jesus," Steve says. "Look at you!"

Mark rubs feeling back into his rotator cuff. There is something not quite healthy about Steve's tan. The tips of Steve's clipped sideburns are edged with gray. Two years ago, they were still in college. Mark regroups. "So where's Danielle?"

Steve's face slackens. "Didn't you read my email? She had to go to a friend's baby shower and catch a later flight. She'll be in at six thirty."

Mark does not remember this email. Email, in general, he dislikes, tends to skim, and quickly deletes, especially those sent by Steve, most of which are nth-forwarded Clinton-hating samizdat.

Steve looks around the lobby, nothing quite managing to catch his attention. Finally, he turns back to Mark. "So what is it you *do* here?"

Mark thinks of the answers, by turns baroque and defensive, he has tailored to answer this question. When your employment is established upon assisting someone, you are gripped by an understandable need to boost the significance of that person. He briefly considers telling Steve that William Stanley Jerome daily absorbs an entire industry's ultraviolet hype and neutralizes it with the sunscreen of responsible criticism. That Jerome is one of the few incorruptible guardians of American letters. Of course, this will mean nothing to Steve. Mark would like to tell Steve what he tells his parents: Jerome runs the review, and the review *matters*. But the review doesn't matter. Not at all. It is barely even a regional phenomenon, three-quarters of its circulation living within a five-mile radius of where Mark now stands. No one reads the thing. Not even Mark really *reads* the thing. What, then, can he tell Steve, who upon first learning of Mark's job confided he had not finished a book since his freshman year of college and had never, as far as he knew, read a novel or a poem?

"I'm the Assistant to the Editor-in-Chief." Mark enunciates so that the Capitals of his Title are Obvious.

Steve's face remains polite. "Okay. And what does *he* do?"

Mark smiles. "Come on, let's get out of here."

In the elevator, on the way down, Steve shakes his head. "So this is New York. This is your job. Your life."

Mark watches descending floor buttons ignite and go dim, the building's elevators so slow that you felt yourself aging while riding them. "Tell me about Houston."

Steve's mouth smooshes over to one side. "Mostly it's good. A lot of Mexicans."

Mark chooses to take this as an inarguable empiricism. The doors open; Mark lets Steve exit first. They walk down a black marble hallway that feels strangely similar to being underwater.

Steve turns to him. "What are you *really* doing at that pissant place? Seriously. Did you go to Yale to make twenty grand a year?"

In a moment of weakness and frustration, Mark had disclosed his salary to Steve during one of the preparatory conversations leading up to this reunion. Steve had, in turn, disclosed his salary, which caused Mark, very briefly, to consider suicide. Startled beads of sweat form on Mark's forehead as they leave the building's igloo-cool air and step into the semitropical haze of Sixth Avenue. "I like what I do."

Steve has the sudden agreeability of a man on the better end of a patently uneven compromise. "Yeah, of course. That's important." Then he looks around. "So *now* what do we do?"

"My place," Mark says. "We'll drop off your stuff."

Without warning Steve marches past Mark toward the curb, a vehement arm up. One fared cab after another barrels past him, uptown.

"I live *down*town," Mark says. "Come on. There's a subway at the end of the block."

"No subways. *I'll* pay for the cab. Don't worry about your candy-ass budget this weekend."

Steve spends the next five minutes perched on the edge of the curb, his arm fruitlessly extended. Mark stands back, wondering if society's safety measure against people like Steve is to lavish upon them salaries that impair true malevolence. It seems to him of sudden, unmistakable historical importance that both Lenin and Hitler were once indigent. Mark looks over to see a cab cutting across Sixth in a great swerving roundelay of horns and brake lights. The taxi angles in on Steve with kamikaze precision before, at the last instant, pulling up to the curb. Steve picks up his suitcase. "Finally!"

The cab is thick with a heavy, roiling stink of incense that goes from unpleasant to intolerable by Thirty-Fourth Street. They finally roll down their windows as the driver manages the tricky right at Twenty-Third and Fifth with suicidal aplomb. At the stoplight on Twenty-Third and Seventh, the cab's idle vibrates their seat. Steve leans back, inspecting Chelsea's pastiche of corporate interests, flyers, brightly colored eateries, and antique shops. "Hey," he says, shooting up straight and pointing.

Mark knows what will be at the other end of Steve's finger even before he looks. Two lean young men in glowing white shirts and black slacks walk hand in hand down Seventh.

Steve's voice lowers to a conspiratorial whisper: "Fudge packers."

Mark looks at Steve in wonder. The cab surges forward. "Right on the next block," he tells the driver.

Mark lives in the one-bedroom basement of a town house owned by a TV personality well known to insomniacs as the host of an all-night news show on one of the network's cable offshoots. He is a friend of Jerome's. This whiff of celebrity impresses Steve, even though he's never heard of the man, his show, or the cable offshoot. They enter through the door beneath the stoop.

The first thing Steve does after leaving his suitcase upright on the floor is kick the leg of Mark's carrot-colored sofa, which Mark rescued from Eighteenth Street after bribing a homeless man to help him lug it home. Steve turns to the rest of the apartment, which is small and dim, enlivened only by a dozen plants in varying stages of decomposition and two large bookcases stuffed with mangled galleys and half-read books. The kitchen is barely a walk-in, much less an eat-in. The bathroom seems like a cell in an unusually bleak prison. The little available daylight beams through a pair of rectangular, sidewalk-level windows in thick motey shafts. Mark activates the air-conditioning, which chokes out a wall-rumbling sputter before kicking in.

"It's small," Steve says, walking around and nodding, "but nice. You found yourself a good little wigwam."

What Mark does not have the heart to tell Steve is that, in order to pay his rent, his parents have reinstated his allowance, though this is strictly an emergency measure lend-lease kind of thing.

They enter Mark's bedroom, Steve's nose scrunching against its etherous, ineradicable stench of mothballs. Mark sits on the lumpy futon while Steve unpacks the many chambers of his suitcase. While making sure everything has remained properly folded, Steve talks about how he met Danielle. Mark stops listening when Steve begins to line up on his bureau an array of pill bottles.

"What's all that stuff?" Mark cuts in, with growing concern.

Steve smiles and underhands to him a small, rattling blue bottle. Mark catches it and reads the label: ENDO-STAK.

"Testosterone supplements," Steve explains. "Both androgenic and anabolic."

Steve wrenches open the accordion door of Mark's closet and hangs a tandem of starched dress shirts beside a tatterdemalion assemblage of Mark's own. When he finishes they retire to the living room, Steve eventually collapsing onto the couch, where he props up both arms on the cushiony backrest, his legs scissored open. Mark sits on the floor, noticing that Steve's forearms very nearly share the same circumference as his biceps. The only places Steve is normally proportioned are his joints, his feet and hands, and his forehead. Steve's skin, where it wraps itself around muscle, has the unhappy distended look of bratwurst boiled too long.

Mark consults his watch. "What time did you say Danielle's plane got in?"

"Six thirty," he says. "When should we leave?"

"Actually, I probably shouldn't." Mark reaches for the Conrad pages and flutters them. "I've got some work I really need to do."

Sunlight angles in through the windows above Steve's head and falls in two rhombi on the carpet. Mark stares at Steve through this soft-focus wall of light. Steve closes his eyes. "Ah. Your work. Your important work."

Mark's heart goes dark and cankered. He wonders how much of Steve's contempt for everything was present in him from conception—jagged links in his polypeptide chain. There was the day Steve turned up at his front door, demanding that he smell his finger after rendezvousing with Kimberly Cooley in a dugout at the ball field down the road. (Mark had smelled it, too.) Or the time they talked a mildly disabled girl named Danielle Ladaris into eating Purina. Or all those boys they'd viciously kidney-punched as they reached up into their lockers, leaving them at the quaking brink of incontinence on the polished hallway floor. Mark is no longer that person. He is no longer beguiled by Steve. But between selves there is always a recognizable perimeter, and Mark suddenly finds himself thinking of a boy named Trevor Travers.

Once, for reasons he has forgotten—it is possible there was no reason—Mark helped Steve chase Trevor into the hilly thatch behind Holy Family after school. Trevor was Steve's favorite quarry because he never did anything Steve could even pretend deserved punishment. He was skinny and shy, all arms and legs, like a human spider. Most of the boys they bullied were pathetic quislings: hours after suffering some humiliation at Mark's and Steve's hands, there they were sliding cookies to them across the table during lunch. But Trevor's distaste for Steve and Mark seemed somehow highborn; they could do nothing to him his inviolate passivity would not void.

In his mind Mark occasionally stumbled upon, and instantly pushed away, memories of the murky, leaden afternoon they chased Trevor into the trees, branches whipping across their faces. When Steve finally tackled the boy and turned him over, Trevor's fear was so thick all Mark could manage was a scared little grin. For a long time Steve sat on Trevor's chest, playfully slapping him across the face. Then, for no reason—Trevor never fought back, never said a word—Steve punched him in the face. As Steve climbed off, Trevor spit up a rheumy throatful of blood onto his Catholic schoolboy's uniform. He began to cry. Steve kicked him, softly at first, then harder, in the ribs. He did this at least a dozen times, until Trevor was weeping so hard his ears went purple with asphyxia. It was horribly thrilling to watch someone wield such control over another. "Go ahead," Steve said to Mark, calmly picking away loose dirt and pine needles from his stained knees. Mark never forgot the expression on Trevor's face as he kicked him. It was, almost, forgiveness.

The next day Trevor's mother appeared in school in her son's place. Steve and Mark were hooked from class and escorted to the principal's office by two skeletal nuns. There Mrs. Travers awaited them, shaking with rage in her stiff, mannish suit. She told them her son cried himself to sleep every night. Cried on his way to school. Cried when he returned home. She did not want Steve and Mark punished, she told them. She simply wanted them to think about this. And Mrs. Travers left, having thoroughly overestimated the power of Steve's conscience. Steve's next punishment, two days later, in gym class, which Mark silently watched with twenty other underwear-clad boys lined up against their lockers, nearly put Trevor Travers in the hospital.

A sortie of priests (one of them a child psychiatrist) descended upon Holy Family. They sequestered Mark to a small room, sometimes with his parents, sometimes not, and asked him questions about Anger. For a while Steve made brash but inconsistent appearances at school but stopped coming altogether when Trevor's family filed assault charges against him. It was said that the charges were dropped at the pleading insistence of Trevor himself. A month later Steve's father moved the family away to Indiana, and though at the time these events all seemed distinct and unconnected, Mark now isn't so certain. Trevor's family moved, too, to Iowa, a little less than a year later.

The room has grown browner, cooler: the air conditioner chugs with diesel enthusiasm.

"You ever think about Flat Rock?" Mark asks suddenly.

Steve's eyes open. He leans forward. "Try not to."

"Do you ever think of—"

"What time is it?" Steve asks, standing, his eyes watery and dim. "Did I fall asleep?"

"It's five o'clock."

Steve takes out his wallet and checks it for ready cash. "Are you coming with me or not?"

"No," Mark says.

Steve walks off to Mark's bedroom, shaking his head. "Where can I catch a cab?"

"Ninth Avenue. Take a right at the sidewalk. It's the first big street you come to."

Steve emerges from the bedroom with his copy of *Muscle & Fitness* and a thin braided belt. "I can't believe you're not coming," he mutters, training the belt through the loops of his slacks. At the door, Steve stops and turns back toward Mark.

Mark's head hurts. He is thirsty. He feels, within him, the static interference between past and present slowly fade away. "What is it?" he asks.

For a moment Steve says nothing. Then: "Know what your problem is? You think too much." He opens the door. "See you in a while, cumstain."

Boom boom. Mark sits up with a jerk, a puffy ache behind each eye. He has no idea how long he's been asleep, how long Steve's been knocking. His watch face is unreadable in the dark. The night beyond his windows is cantaloupe colored by streetlight. Mark turns on a lone-standing lamp to see the Conrad pages strewn across the floor.

As Mark cobbles them together, Steve's knocks grow more forceful. "Quit beating your meat and open the damn door!" When he does, he finds Steve draped with more baggage than a Sherpa. "What the hell took you so long?"

"I fell asleep," Mark admits, still too foggy to lie. Behind Steve, cloaked in shadow, stands a fidgety young woman looking back at the sidewalk.

A disgusted grunt escapes Steve. "Hope you got lots of *work* done." He pushes past Mark and dumps Danielle's stuff in a heap in the middle of the room. He moves into the kitchen and begins, for some reason, to wash his hands. "Delayed, delayed, *delayed!*" he shouts. "For two hours I stared at that goddamn screen. And then—the luggage! And our *damned* cabdriver! Took that ni- took that guy forever. Why the hell didn't you tell me you're at 353 *West* Twentieth Street?"

"Hi," the girl says, stepping inside. Mark stares at her until she nods timidly, prompting him. "I'm Danielle?"

"Oh," he says, shaking her small, bony hand. "Hello."

Mark fights a losing battle at the prospect of once-overing Danielle. He does so quickly, hoping she doesn't notice but knowing women always do. Danielle is wearing a sleeveless viridescent dress that stops just above sculpted kneecaps. She is not attractive, exactly, or beautiful. These words produced inappropriately wholesome referents. Danielle's body is lurid and unreal in the casing of her green dress, with arms and shoulders muscular enough to dismay.

Mark's smile is as false as an emcee's. "Welcome to New York."

"She's never been out of Texas before," Steve says, spinning off the faucet. Somewhere in the walls, the pipes seize. "Can you believe that?"

Mark, who very much could believe that, watches Danielle stomp a sandaled foot against the industrial gray carpet while shooting Steve a fiery yet strangely harmless look. "I have so!"

"Oklahoma doesn't count." Steve stalks across the room in a fullback's half crouch, grasps her around the waist, lifts her off her feet, and spins around as though preparing to shot-put her across the room. Danielle shrieks through drapes of swirling hair, thudding her fists against Steve's back. Satisfied, he sets her down, both of them rouged with exertion.

"It's only ten o'clock," Mark says. "What do you guys feel like doing?"

"Times Square," Steve says instantly. "I wanna see it all lit up at night. Like the movies."

Danielle sucks in a small breath of concern. The strip of skin between her upper lip and nose is waxed and shiny, a hue off from the rest of her face. She looks to Steve, to Mark, to Steve again. "Is that safe? Daddy told me not to go out after dark."

"I *told* you," Steve says heavily. "It's *fine*. Your dad was here for one day twenty *years* ago." Duly chastened, Danielle looks down at her sandals. Steve then turns to Mark. "She doesn't like Houston either. Her hometown has a population of seven."

"So big." Danielle presses her face against the jostling cab's light-plashed window. "Everything is so *big*."

"Oh, come on," Steve says, something nasty lurking beneath the palimpsest of his smile. "Houston's big. Dallas is big. New York's not that different."

Danielle ignores this.

Mark, sitting between them, is too thrilled by the prospect of reality filtered through a non-Steve consciousness to let Danielle remain silent all the way to Times Square. He asks her about her life.

She turns away from the window. "My life?"

Mark wonders if anyone, ever, has asked her such a question. "Your job. Where you grew up. What you like to do."

She is a secretary at Steve's company ("But not Steve's secretary!"), a job she's held since graduating from John Connally High School, where she was captain of the cheerleading squad, four years ago. She is considering going back to school next fall to become an elementary school teacher. Her father is a Methodist pastor, her mother a housewife. And there it is. Danielle's life story has taken them exactly four blocks.

She was really excited to meet Mark, she says, as though just remembering it, after Steve told her about his job. "I *love* to read," she says. "Always got my nose buried in a book." It really *bothers* her that Steve can't bring himself to read. "No time for it," Steve says, watching the storefronts coast past his window. Danielle wants to know: Was he always like this? Mark tells her he thinks so, yes. Danielle sighs and plays with the clasp on her purse. Suddenly: "Do you know Stephen King?"

Mark: "His work. I know his work, sure. *Misery*. Fantastic book."

"But do you know *him*? I figured that since you review books and all you might have met him at a party or something."

"Pretty sure Stephen King lives in Maine," Mark says.

Steve leans forward to look over at Danielle. "You see? I *told* you he wouldn't know him."

Mark sits there, scrunched between their hard, fragrant bodies, piecing together the archaeology of their debates on this strange topic.

"I *love* Stephen King," Danielle says. "My favorite is *The Eyes of the Dragon*. And *The Talisman*. I like it when he tries new stuff."

The cab drops them at Fortieth and Broadway. The high, dominating Coca-Cola sign cycles its programmed drain from fat pixilated red to black and back again. The sky is forbiddingly dark. A descending jet cruises overhead. The streets burn with bonfires of head- and brake lights. Even this far south the streets are thick with bodies. Danielle's face appears both terrified and transfixed.

Mark takes the lead. Steve and Danielle link hands and fall in behind him. Soon they are muscling into the entrails of the neon beast itself. From one canthus to the other Mark's eyeballs are plastered with stimulus, the noise and light grand mal inductive. As Mark pushes through the crowd, he notes that people who do not give way to him are allowing Steve a wide, wary berth. Danielle, close to Steve, earns numerous catcalls from deep within the anonymity of the crowd. The air smells sick with benzene, methane, charred street food, human flesh, sublimated sewage. They find a relatively unpopulated corner at Broadway and Forty-Sixth. Danielle has the edgy look of someone who's just downed a handful of amphetamines. Steve holds her close with his dumb, thick arm.

Mark gestures back at the chaos. "What do you think?"

Danielle, her head set against Steve's shoulder: "It's sad. No one smiles here."

Mark, trying to be cheerful: "Maybe we could go in one of the stores?"

Steve, looking away: "Let's just get the hell out of here."

They walk back down the comparative ghost street of Fifth Avenue. Other than the excitement of traipsing through the shadow of the Empire State Building, Danielle and Steve say nothing to Mark. He leads them by a quarter of a block, his head down. The sidewalk glitters in the moonlight. A countdown now exists in his mind: the number of hours he has left with the Conrad essay Jerome had given him. How many hours did he waste by falling asleep? How, short of origami, will he "make something" of it by Monday? All he managed earlier was some poky, hesitant line work.

Mark looks back at the intersection of Fifth and Thirtieth to see Danielle and Steve whispering and cuddling. So. There you are. Somewhere in his cryogen-filled heart, Steve has the capacity for tenderness. The night is cooling now, the air filled with an almost Aegean temperateness. Mark turns right at Twenty-Third and Fifth, getting as far as the trash-swirling midpoint between Seventh and Eighth, when Steve calls out, "Hey! How about we wet our whistles?"

Mark stops and looks back. Her trauma within Times Square safely in the past, Danielle is all toothy smiles at the thought of a drink. Unfortunately, due both to Mark's ascetic temperament and financial limitations, New York nightlife is a largely undiscovered country to him. He walks back to them. "Sure. What do you have in mind?"

Steve thumbs toward the drinking hole to his immediate right. It is a smallish, chic place, sunken secretively beneath the street. Fernlike greenery shrouds the concrete stairs down to its door. "How about here?"

Mark looks up at the sign. WEST OF SEVENTH. Next to the sign is a rainbow flag. He points. "Just so you know, that's a gay bar."

"A gay bar?" Danielle says with some worry.

Steve lowers into a squat and peers into one of West of Seventh's windows. "No way. I see *three* chicks in there. At least."

"It *looks* like a nice place," Danielle ventures.

"I'm sure it *is* a nice place," Mark tells her.

"There's no *way* that's a gay bar," Steve says.

Mark is so very tired of Steve. "Okay. Then let's go inside."

They pick their way down the steps, enter unnoticed, and stand shoulder to shoulder to shoulder just inside the door. In the soft, warm light, the walnut bar and mirror behind it gleam like freshly polished jewelry. The bartender is a middle-aged man in a bad Hawaiian shirt unbuttoned to his fuzzy sternum. The room is highly segregated, physiology mirroring physiology: the sly and dumpy congregate with the sly and dumpy, the sleek and handsome with the sleek and handsome. The room's two eldest statesmen, silver-haired epicureans in expensive suits, sit next to each other at a small circular table in the corner, sipping martinis: the kind of men who look like they're smoking even though they're not.

Two of the women Steve positive-ID'd are absolutely not women, at least not in terms Steve would accept. One, a heavy blonde with a beehive wig and thick eyeliner, dispenses drinks around the room. The other is a tall, ravishing humanoid sitting alone at the bar, a slim unlit cigarette poised between two fingers. Steve's remaining woman sits with four men. The small segment of bar top she has claimed as her own is littered with glasses slick with pinkish residue. Although no one appears to be listening to her, she is talking at volume and clearly drunk in the joyless manner of someone in relapse.

Mark, his point made, turns to leave. But just as some risible mid-eighties pop erupts from a hidden stash of speakers, Steve plunges deeper into the room. Piqued heads turn to track Steve's progress. Danielle makes quick use of Steve's entry wound in the crowd. Mark follows, but people are actively dancing now, closing off the gaps Steve's path has created. Mark bumps into a freckled man with a periwig of red hair, who gives him an utterly dismissive shin-to-neck appraisal before turning away. The full insult begins to settle in, but suddenly Danielle is pulling on his shirtsleeve: Steve has found a table in back. Chivalrously, Steve pulls out a chair for Danielle and sits beside her, their backs to the room. This leaves Mark with the booth. He sits, running his hands over the smooth black tabletop, in the middle of which tiny candles flicker in testicularly paired glass orbs.

"Okay," Steve says. "Maybe you were right."

The waiter or waitress or whatever the proper term would be approaches their table. Steve orders a Jack and Coke; Danielle an amaretto sour; Mark, inexplicably, a white Russian.

"You know," Steve says while they wait for their drinks, "when you come right down to it, I've really got nothing against fags."

The waiter returns with their drinks, all served in thick tub glasses. Over Steve's objection Mark pays. They toast New York. A new song comes on—some looped sample, wordless and tribal and bare. To the delight of the crowd, two dumpy guys in unashamedly tight shirts grind crotches as though attempting some sort of wool-blend cold fusion.

Danielle has taken one sip from her drink when she sets the glass down and pushes it away. She turns to Steve with a quietly horrified face. "I just realized. Do you think it's safe?"

Steve manages a sober swallow. "Jesus. I didn't even think of that."

Mark stares at them. "Is what safe?"

"The glasses," Steve says. "Drinking from the glasses." He, too, pushes his glass away. "Jesus Christ. They probably got AIDS all over 'em."

A short, bald black man taps Danielle on the shoulder. Danielle turns to him with a petrified squeak. "I just wanted to tell you," the man says, "that your hair is *fabulous*."

Danielle's demeanor changes instantly. Giggling, blushing, she primps herself.

"I'm *serious,*" he says. "I'm a hairdresser. It's marvelous. Gorgeous." He glances at Steve's saturnine face, touches Danielle on the shoulder, and brings his mouth so close to her ear that Mark is certain he is going to kiss her. Instead, he whispers something and quickly twirls away.

Steve half rises from his chair. "What did he say to you?"

Danielle is staring at her reflection in the tabletop, still attempting to process. "He told me to break some . . . *hearts* tonight?"

Now Steve does stand, after which he turns to the room. From the startled slump of his shoulders, it is clear to Mark that Steve has forgotten why, exactly, he stood. The two guys who moments before had been satisfied with frottage are now making out. A few others have paired off, too. The waiter is dancing alone, managing an involved series of pirouettes and turns and vaguely Egyptian hand thrusts.

Danielle turns to look for herself. Within seconds she is gathering up her purse and yanking on Steve's arm. When they hit the street, Danielle cries out, "We were in hell! We were in *hell!*"

Mark leans against the iron balustrade at the top of West of Seventh's stairs, wondering whether he should tell Steve and Danielle that they are walking in the wrong direction.

No sleep. Mark's pillowless night is spent on his couch, but by five a.m. his discomfort has become intolerable, his sheet adhered to his body by now-freezing night sweat. He rises, deactivates the air conditioner, and returns to the couch, his neck spasming and back throbbing in pain. Sometime after eight his sticky bedroom door pops open and discharges Steve, who is wearing only a bright red Speedo. After granting Mark a grouchy nod, he stumbles into the bathroom, where he urinates with great force for at least thirty seconds. Steve then steps back into the living room. "By the way, your room's hotter than the devil's cunt."

Mark looks at Steve standing there in his Speedo and feels a strange impulse to attack him. Last night, in an admirable gesture, Steve left the door open as they all wished one another a good night's sleep. Later Mark awoke to find the door closed. Over the drone of the air conditioner, Mark heard the initially mysterious and then quite familiar wood-on-wood squeak of his futon. Steve was *fucking* Danielle. In his *bed*.

"It might have been cooler," Mark tells Steve evenly, "if you'd left the door open."

Steve's smile is quick and guarded. At that moment Danielle tiptoes out of the bedroom behind him. She has transformed Steve's shirt from last night into discreet morning wear. "Hey, y'all," she says. The early hour finds Danielle's face greasy and pallid, her hair frizzy and damaged looking. Cradled in her arms is a restorative array of soaps, a tube of Aquafresh, bottles of shampoo and hair spray, little plastic seashells of cosmetics, a contact lens case, and a sleek-looking blow dryer. With her rump she knocks shut the bathroom door behind her. Moments later, the showerhead hisses to life.

"So what's on the agenda today?" Steve asks brightly.

"Anything," Mark says. "Whatever."

"There's this clothing store Danielle's all wet about, down by Union Circle."

"Union Square." Mark tries to communicate telepathically how badly he wants Steve to put on some clothes.

"We should check it out first. Just to get it out of the way."

Thirty minutes later Danielle emerges towel-turbaned from her shower and shuttles back and forth from bedroom to bathroom in a series of intermediary outfits. Mark is ready to go in ten minutes, Steve just over twenty. They wait. When Danielle at last steps from Mark's bedroom fully equipped, he and Steve are playing a lethargic game of Go Fish on the couch.

Steve throws down his cards, stands, and looks Danielle over. "I thought you were gonna wear the sundress."

Danielle casts a wounded look down at her Wrangler and tank top ensemble. "I thought I'd wear that out to dinner tonight."

Steve nods curtly. "Then turn around. Lemme see your ass."

The air outside Mark's apartment broils; both ends of the block are watery with mirage. They plunge into the heat, bracing themselves as though against some great apocalyptic wind. Conversation revolves around how genuinely unappealing Steve finds every person they pass until, halfway to Union Square, Danielle decides that it is possible the clothing store she's looking for is actually near *Columbus* Square.

Mark stops and turns to her. "Columbus *Circle*. There is no Columbus Square."

"Oh." Danielle smiles at him.

Mark takes note of Steve's growing anger. "What's the name of this place?" he asks Danielle quickly. "I might know where it is."

"I wrote it down." She mimes the act of writing something down.

Steve's face goes blank with anger. "You left the address back in Houston, didn't you?"

Danielle hides a pink strip of visible bra beneath her tank's shoulder strap. She consults Mark: "We can still find it, can't we?"

"How far's Columbus Circle?" Steve asks the sky.

Mark runs his thumb along his jawline. "About forty blocks from here."

"Jesus *fuck*."

"We can *find* it," Danielle says. "*Mark* can find it."

Mark guides them down Seventeenth Street and stops at the crosswalk where the toxic, traffic-choked flume of Broadway is forced athwart at Union Square. He points out to no one in particular how Union Square's stately perimeter of buildings seems peristylar, classical, one last surge of grid logic before the city succumbs beneath Fourteenth Street to mostly number-less chaos. Danielle and Steve look around numbly. Couples sharing ice-cream cones abound. The tables of the half dozen outdoor cafés are packed. Mark cuts over to the sidewalk border-ing the park, whose dime-bag-vending brigands blithely ignore Giuliani's edict that they cease to exist. At the art deco subway kiosk at the corner of Union Square West and Fourteenth Street, Steve turns on Danielle with sudden ferociousness.

"So where's the store, Danielle? Where's the goddamn store? Christ! You always do this shit!"

Through no design of his own, Mark finds himself horned in between them. "*Steve,* what the fuck? Take it easy!"

Steve moves three steps away and whirls around. "You don't understand. It's over and over again." He looks back at Danielle. "What did we talk about? What did we talk about before taking this trip?"

Danielle stares at the sidewalk. She seems not to have heard him.

"Answer me."

"Responsibility," Danielle says quietly. "We talked about re-sponsibility."

Steve's voice lowers to a gentle, almost instructive pitch. "Wasting half a day looking for an address you forgot to bring—does that seem responsible to you?"

Danielle's hands lift in some helpless attempt at defiance.

"Ashley said the store's on Broadway, a few blocks south of Columbus Square—"

"This is *Union* Square!"

She looks away, then, her eyes blurred with two unspilled tears.

Steve turns to Mark. "Fuck all this. Let's grab something to eat."

Mark stands a few conscious feet away from them, in a forceful daze. "You want to eat?"

"Duh. It's lunchtime." As Steve looks around, Danielle approaches him and takes his hand, running her fingers along his arm. "What're the options?"

Mark is still trying, for some reason, to be helpful. "Uh, okay. You like Brazilian?"

Danielle opens her mouth just as Steve says, "No."

"Greek?"

"No."

Mark regards him suspiciously. "Ever *had* Greek?"

"No."

"How about Japanese?"

"We just had Chinese on Thursday."

"They're completely different cuisines."

Steve waves this off. "Let's just start walking. *I'll* find something."

When they come out the opposite side of Union Square, Danielle points at the tall, narrow Barnes & Noble on Seventeenth. "Oh! A bookstore! Can we go inside?"

Mark fears this will set off another detonation, but Danielle knows Steve's pressure points far better than he. "Yeah," Steve says suddenly, pulling her along, "but only for a minute."

They enter together, each using a different door, and are

greeted by the clean, bouncy sound of Vivaldi or perhaps Saint-Saëns. Milling about the cavernous ground floor are mostly women and the store's harried, dashing-about employees. Registers blip and bing over the stately murmur of conversation. Pages turn. Somewhere back in the children's section comes laughter of indeterminate gender. Off to the right, a silent escalator lifts its human cargo upstairs. The air has a faint urinal-cake sweetness.

"Where are the magazines?" Steve asks Mark.

"Third floor."

"Solid copy." Steve heads off toward the escalator.

Mark makes his way over to the New in Paperback table and sees that a history of the Bauhaus has in its trade paperback incarnation culled some front-cover copy from the review's obligatorily mixed review. What he recalls as something along the lines of "an impressive, flawed examination that will be greeted by less informed readers as a valuable addition to its field" has been reborn as "Impressive. . . . A valuable addition to its field."

Danielle is a few tables away, picking over trade paperback fiction. Mark watches her attentively read each back cover, set the book down, and move on to the next. He tells her he is going upstairs and rides the escalator's metal wave up to the second floor. He wanders back into the silence of the shelves, alongside History, around Current Events, through Drama, feeling curiously diminished, as he always did, in the face of so many never-read pages.

He stops in the Philosophy section, three long rows tucked away in back. Mark eyeballs the spines of humanity's attempt to make sense of itself. He plucks Nietzsche's *Beyond Good and Evil* from the shelves. He scans its pages, extracting sentences that beg misapplication when standing alone: "Beware of the martyrdom of knowledge." "Independence is for the very few;

it is the privilege of the strong." "Terrible experiences pose the riddle whether the person who has them is not terrible." "One is best punished for one's virtues." He stops at this: "'The consequences of our actions take hold of us, quite indifferent to our claim that meanwhile we have 'improved.'" He stuffs the book back into place and walks to the shelf's far end, halting at the irregularly alphabetized *A*s. Aristotle. Althusser. There. Arendt. He does not glance at the title of the book he grabs. He simply opens it and reads: "The sad truth of the matter is that most evil is done by people who never made up their minds to be or do either evil or good."

"*There* you are."

He looks up blinkingly from his book. It is Danielle, smiling. "What are you doing back here?"

"Nothing," he says, putting the Arendt back. "Just reading."

Danielle shifts her weight from one foot to the other. "I figured you'd be somewhere like this. Or in poetry." Her face brightens. "You know who writes good poetry? Jewel, surprisingly enough."

Mark is startled by this "surprisingly enough." Doesn't that . . . well, doesn't that suggest *taste*? "Jewel the singer? From Alaska?"

"Uh-huh. We'd better go. Steve's waiting for us downstairs."

Mark has a sudden, impossible vision of educating this girl. Transforming her inchoate suspicion that Jewel should not write good poetry into an adamantine certainty that Jewel *does* not write good poetry. (Then again, Mark has never read Jewel's poetry. Maybe it *was* good.) How easy it would be to sneak Danielle past the checkpoints designed to bar good Christian girls from the halls of culture. The catch is that he wants her obdurately unchanged. He wants her tanned and hard-bodied while they loiter in the Frick, attend experimental plays, share appetizers in French restaurants alongside the human statues of the Upper East Side. He wants to hear her uncultured, melodious voice say, "DeLillo's best novel is *Libra,* easily."

Mark blurts out, in an unpunctuated rush, "Hey do you wanna go to a museum?"

Danielle's head draws back. "You mean, like, pictures?"

"Paintings," Mark says. "Sculpture. Tapestries."

As Danielle smiles, her eyes roll. "You know *he* won't want to, right? Steve never wants to do anything cultured."

"Museum?" Steve says skeptically, when they join him outside.

Danielle presses herself against him like a starveling child. She squeezes his forearm, her red fingernails standing out against his tanning-bed skin. "It'll be fun, baby. Please?"

Steve smirks in a faintly perverse way. Then he shakes his head. "All right. After lunch. But they better have interesting shit."

The museum: it bestrides its six blocks with a timelessness that seems geological. Once inside, Danielle looks up in awe at the Great Hall's vaulted ceiling. Mark leads them into the auburn light of the Egyptian wing, having already compiled a private list of the exhibits he will not, under any circumstances, allow Steve to see: The Arts of Africa, Oceania, and the Americas; Musical Instruments; Asian Art; the Costume Institute. He will provide Steve with no cause to complain. The rest of their afternoon will be without incident. And so they move in a unified column down the Egyptian wing's wide hallway, passing gray friezes, glass cases of trinkets dug up along the Nile, cracked corbels, tattered russet papyruses, birdlike gods. Mark is heartened that they neither linger nor hurry. At the same time, he knows sarcophagi and

Ptolemaic statuary will not hold Steve's interest for long. Suddenly, Danielle stops at a statue of Anubis, the jackal god, his pointy ears broken off. She turns to Steve and smiles. "He's kind of cute."

Steve takes a deep breath and looks around. "I don't get it," he says. "I just don't get any of this."

Mark is a few paces from them, staring at a large pale stone sketched with faded hieroglyphics. He takes note of the individual icons: a staff, an eye, an ankh, something that resembles a tuning fork. Conceivably he could be taught what they all mean. He could learn to scan the message staring back at him. A man with whom he shares a common language and history stands so close to Mark that he can smell his sticky-sweet deodorant, and yet this man seems less penetrable than the weirdo glyphs of a death-obsessed, cat-worshipping culture from which he is separated by four millennia.

"Come on," Mark says. "I'll show you my favorite place."

They enter the Temple of Dendur. The room that holds the temple is as huge as an empty hangar, the ceiling fifty feet high. One wall is all gridded glass, filled with the explosive green foliage of Central Park and a soundless blare of blue sky. In the middle of the room, surrounded by a pool of glittering black water, stands the temple itself. It is small, as temples go, little more than a pile of lumpily eroded stones. But there it is, torn from time, a baton ripped from one culture to another in a two-thousand-year-long relay. Part of what Mark likes about the temple is how sparsely the museum has attempted to re-create a convincingly Egyptian milieu. Other than some statues of cat-faced gods, a few cobra-hooded Tuts, and half a dozen palm trees, it is just the temple in here and the temple alone.

"What the hell *is* this?" Steve asks.

Mark, mistaking Steve's tone for awe, begins to excitedly

enumerate the temple's history. Danielle quickly interrupts him: "I think we'd rather look at some *pictures*."

Mark abandons any educational pretense. He follows them silently as Danielle and Steve drift with blasé hurry through rooms of armor, medieval Christian icons, and decorative art. Danielle spends more time commenting on other women's shoes than anything, and after a while Mark suspects their path through the museum is being determined solely by Steve's subtle stalking of a buxom Scottish girl in tight canvas shorts.

They take a time-out in a long white antechamber of Greek statues, potted trees, and hard iron benches. Danielle and Steve sit together, hands on thighs, while Mark walks figure eights through art students furiously sketching on large pads.

"Oh, man—I almost forgot to tell you," Steve suddenly calls to him, his voice sounding throughout the space. "You know who I saw two weeks ago?"

Mark looks over his shoulder at Steve. "No, I don't know who you saw two weeks ago. How could I?"

"Trevor Travers."

Mark's neural net sawtooths at the sound of this name. He turns to Steve fully. "What?"

"At an airport. In Omaha. I was there on business, waiting at my gate, and who walks right past me? Trevor fucking Travers."

"Who's Trevor Travers?" Danielle asks.

"A guy we went to Catholic school with," Steve tells her.

Mark asks, "You're sure it was him?"

Steve makes a face. "It was him. Trust me. Oh! And get this. He was with a *woman*. I'm not kidding. They were arguing or something. She was arguing, at least. He was just walking, head down, totally ignoring her. I didn't blame him. She looked like a hag."

"Stop it," Danielle says, irritated now. "You're being crude." She pauses. "Did you say anything to him?"

"Was going to." Steve shakes his head. "Didn't seem worth it."

Mark stares at him closely. Was that regret?

"Why?" Danielle asks Steve, grinning. "Were you mean to him?" She turns to Mark. "I bet Steve was mean to him."

Some of the art students have stopped sketching their statue of Poseidon and are now merely standing there, pencils frozen, listening.

"Steve used to beat him up," Mark says, looking at Danielle. "Me, too. I did it, too. His mother came to school once and asked us to stop. She was in tears about it. I felt so horrible, watching this woman—this *mom*—cry. So I stopped. But Steve? Nope. Steve there kept on going." Mark stares at his old friend. "That last time—you broke his nose, didn't you?"

Steve, hunched over, staring at the floor, says nothing.

On the bench she shares with Steve, Danielle scoots imperceptibly away. "Is that true?" she asks him.

Steve glances over at her, shrugs.

Mark presses on: "Steve and I would just . . . pick out certain kids, I guess you'd say. Not because they'd done anything to us; most of them were scared to death of us. Then we 'punished' them. Don't ask me why. Maybe Steve knows."

No one speaks for a moment. Danielle looks at the side of Steve's face as though willing him to turn to her. At last she asks him, "*Do* you know?"

Steve: "Do I know what?"

"Why you did that."

Steve's apparently sincere consideration of Danielle's question concludes with a small, humorless chuckle. Then he rises, pulling Danielle's arm. But she sits a moment, looking at Steve, before standing to join him.

Modern art. Steve chuckles at Georgia O'Keeffe's yonic *Grey Line with Lavender and Yellow,* sneers at Clyfford Still's ambitious ink blots, dismisses Ellsworth Kelly's *Spectrum V.* After an hour of wandering the museum's warrens and hallways, they begin to backtrack. Eventually, Mark finds himself standing before Jacques-Louis David's *The Death of Socrates.* Despite the crash course working at the review has given him in painting, music, architecture, and history—the disciplines literature both robbed and attended—Mark has no special knowledge of art. Some scholar would no doubt be able to explain how *The Death of Socrates* is emblematic of a certain school of French romanticism and therefore not very remarkable. Even Mark's untrained eye can detect the painting's stillborn melodrama. The painting is actually fairly simple. In it, Socrates declaims while reaching for a chalice of hemlock, his punishment for denying the existence of the gods. Socrates's expression is redoubtable, stern. All around him are curly-haired disciples in sherbet-colored robes, some in despair, others resigned, at the prospect of their master's suicide. At the foot of Socrates's bed ("either Xenophon or Plato," according to the accompanying plaque) sits a man in head-bowed contemplation. An empty scroll and inkwell are scattered uselessly at his feet: the master's last words will go unrecorded. Mark stands for minutes staring at this painting until Steve and Danielle saunter up alongside him.

"What's this?" Steve asks. Before Mark can answer, Steve leans toward the plaque and reads: *"The Death of Socrates."* He steps back, nodding. "Didn't know Socrates was so jacked."

"It's not a portrait," Mark says hoarsely.

Danielle, though, agrees with Steve. "His arms are cut real nice."

Mark looks at them both, contemplating the many things of which one would have to be completely ignorant to confuse this painting with portraiture: Greek history, art history, history.

"It's not a fucking portrait!" The gallery's sudden silence allows Mark to realize that he has just shouted. He feels the psychic burden of twenty pairs of shocked eyes. A nearby guard in a navy suit takes a measured step toward him.

Danielle's hand is plastered over her mouth, her eyes filled with little cyclones of surprise. Steve's body is rigid, but he reaches out for Mark, his face full of real concern. "Hey, man. You okay?"

Mark backs away from him. "Don't touch me."

Steve's hand remains suspended there between them. "Don't 'touch' you? Dude, what is your problem?"

Mark feels light-headed, agreeably out of control. "You don't know, do you? You really have no idea." He is shouting again, his voice kicking up gravel in his throat. "You don't even *know*!"

"I know you're acting crazy. I know you're scaring Danielle."

Mark takes a step toward Steve—to do what, he is not certain. He is hoping momentum will determine his action. As Mark nears Steve he notices him looking with worry over Mark's shoulder. Mark glances back just as a guard's large hand lands on his deltoid. The guard is an older man, with big heavy jowls and pouched eyes. He asks Mark if he'd like to get "some air." Mark pushes the man's hand away. Two other guards—and where did *they* come from?—are now taking hold of Mark's arms. After some silently energetic struggle, the guard behind Mark reconfigures his come-along hold into a strangling full nelson. Mark feels the vertiginous rush of his instinctively kicking feet leave the floor before coming down hard again. Danielle is saying something, moving toward Mark, but Steve holds her back. Blood gurgles helplessly at the place in Mark's neck where the guard's arm has tightened. He stops struggling only when Steve, at long last, turns away.

Love Story, with Cocaine

The thing was Maarit didn't even *want* a dog. Her father, though, had insisted. "Maybe," he told her, when he dropped the dog off, "it'll give you something to do." It was true that Maarit did not have much to do, though she always *felt* busy, which was, perhaps, a natural consequence of waking up daily at 3:00 p.m. Most of her activities involved spending her father's money. That her father's solution to this would mean Maarit necessarily spending more of his money (on dog food, on dog toys, on dog hospitals and dog vacations) was typical of him.

Mimu the greyhound came to Maarit already named and fully grown. He moved with snakelike grace. His coat was a rich thunderhead gray and his eyes little expressive bogs of brown. There was, however, no way around the fact that there was something plainly *wrong* with Mimu. He shivered constantly, for one thing, and was such a reflexive biter that Maarit removed Mimu's muzzle only when serving him supper. Soon enough Mimu's most spectacular behavioral quirk emerged: attacking strangers.

The first victim was an old Russian woman, whose mauling occurred within Toompark only a week after Maarit's father first handed her Mimu's leash. In Maarit's mind, the old Russian woman sort of asked for it by dint of attempting to pet Mimu as she passed by. One might think that a leashed, muzzled dog would be incapable of inflicting much damage, but Mimu's previous custodian had not thought to trim his nails in some time—if

89

he or she ever did. By the time Mimu had the old woman on the ground (Maarit pulling back on the leash with every one of her 105 pounds), he was raking her chest and arms with a catlike avidity. It was a cloudy weekday evening; the park was virtually empty. Taking note of this, Maarit helped up the speechless and pretty badly bleeding old woman and without another word allowed Mimu to drag her back to her apartment in the Old Town. For several days she stayed away from Toompark.

The second attack was trickier, emotionally speaking, in that it involved a child who was walking with his mother along Toompark's edge. Again it was early evening, the champagne-colored sun dissolving behind some trees. Mimu just *bolted* at the sight of the boy. The leash in Maarit's hand went from a dense fabric cool to searingly hot in the space of half a second. Maarit let go, endured the endless seconds in which Mimu approached his target, and watched with fascinated horror as Mimu launched himself at the boy like a gorgeous living torpedo. Mimu was still muzzled and Maarit got him under control quickly enough; crystal-eyed shock seemed to be the worst of the boy's injuries. When Maarit tried to slip away, the boy's hysterical mother followed her. When Maarit began to run, so did the mother. Maarit surrendered to her fate and—nodding, apologizing—gave the boy's mother a fake cell phone number and fake address.

Unfortunately for Maarit, the woman knew who she was: Maarit's father, a businessman whose business he chose to describe publicly only as "business," was often in the tabloids. The next day the woman showed up at her apartment with two frowning policemen. (The woman had been provided with Maarit's address by a dry cleaner they both shared, a breach of trust so severe that Maarit seriously considered taking legal action.) When Maarit was asked by the policemen if Mimu had had anything to do with an attack on a Russian woman a few days before, she hesitated a moment too long. They seemed to know her eventual denial was a lie, and there was some vague talk of putting Mimu down. Her father, who had key allies among the city's constabulary, took care of the matter and even gave Maarit money for a dog walker. Maarit hated this taciturn flunky and, after a few weeks, paid the dog walker twice what her father was paying him (three times what her father was paying him, actually, given that it was all his money) to stay away from her. From there she went back to walking Mimu on her own.

The next person Mimu attacked was also in Toompark, this time in the middle of the afternoon. The reason it happened was that Maarit allowed herself to be distracted by the wolf whistle of three Russian men evidently enjoying a midday vodka blowout. When Maarit, whose postindependence command of Russian had faded to a few lush profanities, turned to tell the men to go fuck their mothers with a broken broomstick, Mimu bolted. His victim this time, thank God, was a man. By the time Maarit had Mimu under control (a very relative concept with Mimu, true), the man was, somehow, *laughing* as he got to his feet.

He was an American, maybe in his mid-thirties, and had long and shinily unclean hair: the haircut of someone who did not worry about haircuts. His face, though, was clean-shaven and kind, if not particularly remarkable. He was wearing a black V-neck sweater (which had spared his arms the brunt of Mimu's claws) and jeans whose knees where now whorled with grass stains. Maarit, who had lived for a time in Cambridge before flunking out of school, had always been fascinated by the masculinity gap between the English words *guy* and *man*. Before her was a guy. To her frequent emotional sorrow, Maarit was most often attracted to guys, though she was not attracted to this guy. She did, however, like the fact that he was daring enough to pet Mimu, whose downturned head was so narrow that his dark black nose resembled the dot beneath an exclamation point. To Maarit's surprise, Mimu did not resist the American's touch. Not even a growl.

"What name?" he asked Maarit in her language, which he obviously spoke only in brain-damaged form.

She told him, in English.

"What's it mean?"

"Nothing," she said. "It's his name."

He lowered into a squat to look Mimu in the eye. "Mimu the mean," he said. Apparently this gratified Mimu, who seemed to relax a little, even going so far as to sit, his head lifting in that arrogant greyhound way. The guy looked up at Maarit, squinting. "And what's your name?"

She told him.

He smiled. "All the girls' names here are so pretty."

Maarit was annoyed now. "Do you want something?"

He shrugged. "Everything I want, I've got."

At this, Maarit tried not to smile. Displays of confidence, even when boldly affected, were one of her weaknesses. "You talk like an idiot."

"I'm not a tourist," he said. "I know who you are. We actually live three doors away from each other."

She did not respond. If this was a line, Maarit would give him nothing.

"I'm in eight Rataskaevu. Top floor. You're twelve. No idea what floor you live on."

"Top floor."

"Aren't we both fancy?"

She started away; the guy stood.

"Hey," he said, keeping pace beside her, "your dog attacked me. The least you can do is join me for a drink. My name's Ken."

"You want to drink in the afternoon?"

"I *often* drink in the afternoon."

She looked at him. Her decision wheel spun around inside her and stopped, decisively. "Where?"

"Eight Rataskaevu happens to have an excellent bar."

She laughed. "I'm not going to your apartment."

"I've got other things there. Fun things. Fun things for fancy people."

She said nothing, slightly and suddenly afraid of him now.

He sighed, picked a piece of grass from his sweater, rolled it into a ball, and flicked it away. "Look. You're friends with Jaanus Kask, right?" He looked around, as though invoking this name had been unwise. "Well, I know him, too."

Jaanus Kask was someone Maarit saw fairly frequently, though he was hardly her favorite person on this earth. She liked very much what he was able to get for her, though.

"I don't like doing coke alone," Ken said.

Funny thing: neither did Maarit.

Eight Rataskaevu, recently gutted and diligently renovated, had been built in the fifteenth century. This was something, Ken told Maarit, that he had "tried and failed to give a shit about." She was following him up a spiral staircase whose popping, creaking floorboards seemed vaguely in danger of exploding beneath their weight. They passed four other apartments, one for each of the building's floors, all presently unoccupied. Only a year ago these apartments were going for two thousand euros a month; Ken was paying half that. "I don't know why people are complaining about the economy," he said, opening his door for her. "For me it's been one pleasant surprise after another."

Maarit hesitated. Although neither she nor her family was suffering, a quarter of the city's restaurants had gone out of business in the last four months and so had half its nightclubs. Many of her friends had worked for, and in some cases even owned, those tragedies. She felt a new dislike of him carefully arrange itself in her mind.

Which was obvious, it seemed. He drew back and put his hands up and said, melodically, "Joking, joking." Then he waved her and Mimu into his apartment.

It was a nice space: parquet floors (Mimu's nails!), exposed wooden rafters, and an oak column of obscure utility standing fat and polished in the middle of the enormous room. *Space* was the operative word here: she stood at the edge of a hauntingly unfilled excess of it. When she turned and asked him how long he had been living here, the echo startled her. He claimed to have been here for six months. She took in the apartment's barrenness, trying to imagine its congregation points, its purlieus. There was exactly one: a black leather couch against the far wall, beneath huge curtain-pulled windows. To the right was a weight bench from which hung many articles of drying laundry. She initially missed the windshield-sized flat-screen television mounted upon an exposed rafter high above the couch. Along the wall to her left was a rather beautiful wooden staircase, which, she guessed, led to an upper-floor bedroom. And that was about it, other than the oak-topped kitchen island right in front of her, upon which was a frying pan distinguished by its contents of four or five grams of chunky, unbroken cocaine. A Selver (her nation's largest chain grocery store) preferred-customer credit card lay next to the frying pan, its edge crusty with powder. That, and the spillover coke scattered on the countertop, suggested a man in possession of more coke than he knew what to do with. Maarit had been trying to cut back. Being awake for forty hours and asleep for twenty was fine if you lived alone, but she had Mimu to worry about now. She had slipped twice this month, both times at Club Privé, where doing coke was mandatory, but she had not purchased any for herself in weeks. It was only when she looked into the pan, and felt her throat insidiously parch, that she realized how much she had been missing it.

Ken instantly went to work, isolating two large chunks and chopping away at them with his Selver card. When that was done he scraped toward the center of the pan the stranded perimeter coke his initial chopping had caused to spark away. He managed his lines with precision, pulverizing the coke down to its molecules. A minute later, he had convened ten lines of beautifully daunting girth.

"Why don't you have a mirror?" Maarit asked him, undoing Mimu's leash. Mimu ran about the empty room with a crazed explorer's excited unfamiliarity. She winced at the frantic, scrapy sound his nails made against the parquet. Ken, occupied with rolling up a twenty-euro note, did not notice.

"What do you mean?" he asked.

She pointed at the frying pan and made an I-don't-know-what expression.

Still rolling the twenty, he looked at the frying pan himself. "I guess I didn't buy a mirror because I don't know how to say *mirror*."

"*Peegel.*"

"I was kidding."

"So you can speak a little?"

"I was kidding that it ever occurred to me to buy a mirror."

He smiled at her, crookedly. "You don't like the old magic frying pan trick?"

"It's a little strange."

He handed her the twenty, which, she had to admit, was tremendously well rolled. "Please," he said grandly. "Your dance with the white lady."

She worked the dense little paper tube between her fingers before handing it back to him. "I must be honest with you. I never use money for this."

"How come?"

"Hepatitis?"

Mimu, having finished exploring the room, now sat at Ken's feet, shivering. Ken looked down at him.

"You've never heard about this?" she asked.

He was petting Mimu. "Not once. Not ever."

She felt bad, suddenly, for causing him such consternation. "Well, this is what they say. The hepatitis gets on the money."

"And I say that seems like something I should have known." He looked around.

She wondered, suddenly, how long he had been awake and reached for the twenty. "Give it to me. It's fine."

"No, no. I don't want either of us getting hepatitis. The problem is I don't have anything else handy. You don't have a tooter on you, by any chance, do you?"

She had never heard the word *tooter* before, but its meaning was clear from context. She had one, of course, disguised as a small antique fountain pen. She reached in her purse, popped out the nib, and shook free the hidden silver straw inside.

"Fancy," he said approvingly.

She leaned over the frying pan, blocked one nostril, and with thrilling velocity took in one line, another. She straightened up, sniffing hard (she hated this part and kept her back to him for most of it), and waited. She laughed once, chemically. Most certainly this was the coke of Jaanus Kask. In a city of Russian-cut cocaine—which is to say cocaine that was 90 percent laxative, 9 percent amphetamine, and 1 percent cocaine—Jaanus's refusal to go through the usual Russian providers was a large part of his business model. This kept his coke as clean and unstepped on as possible. With a rush of translucent, unspeedy clarity, she licked her finger, touched it to the frying pan's surface, and rubbed the meager payload against her gums. Within seconds her mouth turned numb and porcelain. She turned to Ken. "How do you know Jaanus?"

"May I?" he asked, gesturing toward her silver tooter. She gave it to him. He followed her lead: two lines, both in quick succession. When he looked at her again his eyes were radiant and a little bulb of moisture glistened in his left nostril. "You asked me something?"

"Jaanus," she said.

"Ah. Met him through a friend—at BonBon, I think? It's a bit foggy."

Mysteriously, he had not yet kissed her. "I'm not sure Jaanus *has* any real friends," she said, trying to be enigmatic.

"Jaanus makes me nervous. The thing about coke is you're never that far away from the man with the gun."

"I don't understand." Frustrated, and a little hurt, she took the silver straw from him and did another line, heedlessly.

He stepped back to give her room. "When you're buying weed, or even pills, the guy with the gun is pretty far away. You've got at least a dozen people between you and the guy with the gun. With coke, you're no more than two or three people away from the guy with the gun. With Jaanus I feel like I'm only one person away from the guy with the gun."

This was absurd. Jaanus Kask was very smart and a liar and terrible in bed, but he was not violent. Or maybe Ken knew him in a different, more accurate context. Then again, she often found that the world was capable at any given moment of undermining the integrity of her basic impressions—a central personal anguish. Mimu, for instance. She looked at her sweet boy now, still peacefully sitting at the feet of a man he did not even know. Why would Ken not kiss her?

"Maybe I'm wrong about Jaanus," Ken said thoughtfully. "I don't know. But here—let's go do something."

She followed him to the couch, which was so soft and deep one did not sit on it so much as unconditionally surrender to it. She hoped her breath was okay. But again he did not kiss her. Instead, from beneath the couch, he pulled out some kind of American board game, which was called Operation. Ken thought it would be fun to play in their condition. Maarit's molars were now seeking contact with her brain. What on earth was he doing? What on earth was *she* doing? Maarit politely waited for Ken to say more about the game, but he did not. Thirty seconds passed. "Let me go get the pan," he finally said.

As he walked across the room to fetch his cocaine she sunk deeper into the couch, feeling erotically shapeless. The couch leather smelled cold and synthetic. When Ken returned with the pan he did another two lines, set the pan on the floor, and opened the game box. Now this was the most ridiculous thing: Ken handed Maarit a pair of tiny tweezers, which were connected to the flimsy plastic game board by a thin black wire. "There's sup-posed to be cards," Ken said, "but I have no idea where they are. Other than that the game's pretty self-explanatory."

"This man," Maarit said, "looks like Boris Yeltsin."

Ken took a newly intrigued look at the red-nosed patient on the game board. "Holy moly. He does."

She set the tweezers aside. "I'm not playing your stupid Yel-tsin game." She then looked across the room. Mimu was in one of its emptily dark corners, his haunches trembling and his face turned to the wall as he pushed out a considerable turd.

Ken, noticing Mimu himself, returned the game to its box

and said, "Your dog just shat on my floor." He stood and made his way over to ground zero. Once he had Mimu's leavings safely contained in a great bouquet of paper towels, he asked Maarit to open the window behind her. She refused and told him to throw it in the toilet, but Ken said he thought that would be "weird." So she opened the window and Ken threw the towels and the mess out and into the alley below. They did the rest of the lines and decided to hold off making any more for at least ten minutes. Three minutes later, they made more lines.

"What do you do?" she asked him, as he finished.

Another practiced sigh escaped him. "Right now, you're kinda looking at it."

"And you live here?"

"I do."

"For how long?"

"Six months, like I said."

"I mean to ask how long will you live here?" Maarit could not believe she had asked him this. It was a signal she was already thinking of him in an expectational way, which she was not. The waft of Mimu's leavings still lingered within the room like a terrible curse.

Ken set the pan on the floor and said, "I have no idea how long I'll live here. Until I get tired of it, I guess."

"So you came to my country to do cocaine all day long? Couldn't you do that in America?"

"I *was* doing that in America. One day I literally googled 'beautiful cities' and all of a sudden I was looking at Saint Olaf's Church. Did you know that for, like, five minutes in the fifteenth century it was the tallest structure in Europe?"

Maarit had never heard that before. "Who said this?"

"Wikipedia. And now I live right down the street from Saint Olaf's Church. I moved here because it was beautiful."

"Where did you live before coming here?"

"The Pacific Northwest."

She had never heard of it. "Is that America?"

"Yeah."

"Where is it?"

"On the Pacific. In the northwest."

"More coke." She bent over to fetch the pan.

He stopped her, his hands fitting comfortably around her shoulders. They were pleasant hands, firm but not at all grabby. "Don't. Not yet. It's nice having you here. Can I touch your arm?"

"You smell like a dog shit."

"The entire room smells like a dog shit. So can I?"

"Kiss me first."

He made a small, frustrated, vowely sound. An unsilent quiet descended upon them. The coke had made Maarit's mind a factory of incomplete frustrations. English got away from her, too, her nimble mind running for speed while her laggard mouth jogged and gasped behind it. The silence, though, was helpful, in that it reminded her she knew nothing of this man, this guy, who was living in her country with the apparent sole purpose of doing drugs. She should leave now. But she had a weakness for foreigners. There was the Englishman (many Englishmen), the Frenchman, the Swede, the Arab, the Canadian. All had left her with a diverse arrangement of wounds. It was always the same: she loved what two people from different places could not know about each other, enjoyed figuring out what this allowed her to hide, until the final, sad discovery that it allowed them to hide just as much, if not more. Finally, she said, "I think this is a very expensive apartment. For most of us, it's expensive. What do you do here?"

"I'm here to write, but I'm not doing much of it."

"Write," she said.

He misunderstood her confusion as an invitation to explain. "I want to write about interesting people, but the only things I ever write are about writers. When I read books or stories about writers it makes me crazy. It's like: *Again, dude? Seriously?* But at a certain point, as a writer, you forget about what having a job and going to work actually feels like. And so you start imagining someone who has no responsibility to anyone but himself. To avoid making him a writer you start coming up with the weirdest imaginable jobs. Which is no better than writing about writers."

Maarit had not read a book in at least two years, though she had read a lot as a girl. Enough, at least, to confirm that she did not enjoy reading. She did not mind books and abstractly admired those people who chose to read them, but if Friday night rolled around and her only choices were to read or to sit and stare at a wall she was not certain what she would do. It was amazing she had lasted at Cambridge as long as she did. "So you're a writer?"

"That really depends on where you stand on some key aesthetic issues."

"I didn't understand."

"I write. Am I writer? I don't know."

He was boring her a little. "So you write . . . books?"

"Trying. I used to write video games. The dialogue, at least. That's how I made my money." Now he was rubbing her shoulders, possibly a little too hard, but she did not mind. "I will assume you don't play."

"Never," she said. She could not think of a single video game. No, wait. She had one. The little yellow man, who ate the dots.

"My college roommate went to work for a video game company. A small one, at the time. Later, he remembered what I used to write in college, and how much he liked it, and asked me to come up with some stuff the game's characters would say to each other during combat. These are called 'barks.' Apparently I write really good barks, because the next thing I knew I was helping out with the script for the rest of the game. I also bought some stock in the company, which turned out to be the smartest thing I've ever done."

Maarit's roommate at Cambridge had been a Frenchman. A Frenchguy, more precisely. A student. Also a cocaine dealer. She blamed the Frenchguy, sometimes, for her flunking out. "Who was the little yellow man, the man who ate the dots?"

"Pac-Man. This was a totally different sort of game. So the first thing they told me was that they wanted a realistic, serious story. This was sort of a problem because the game was about shooting aliens that bleed purple blood. Then they told me, 'We want this game's dialogue to be mysterious. Invent a bunch of technological things the characters can talk about. They don't have to make sense.' I turned out to be good at that, too. At one point, really deep into the development cycle, we realized we didn't actually have a story. What we had was a bunch of guys fighting aliens in slightly different situations. So I was then asked to add what was called an 'emotional core' to the story. Is this boring you, by the way?"

"I don't understand a thing you're talking about."

"I'll speak slower. So. I added a love interest. A girl. It was decided that this girl would represent truth. Or goodness. Whatever. She got cut. I think my proudest moment was when I came up with the name of the alien plan: the Zero Endeavor. Everyone *loved* it. It was a special pleasure of mine that I had no idea what the Zero Endeavor meant. No one else did either. What it basically did was make a sequel necessary and ensure that I had a job writing it."

"Do you have your Zero game here?"

"I do, but that's not what it's called. It's called *ShatterGate*.

The sequel is *ShatterGate Strike: Scoured Lands*. Not my titles. The sequel was the one I made the real money on. It sold six million copies and the company went through the roof. I cashed out with what seemed like a whole lot of money. Then I started doing coke."

"I want you to kiss me," she said.

He released her shoulders and she turned to look at him. His hair remained appalling, but his eyes were beautiful, lit from behind by some narcotic, diamond light. He wanted to kiss her, she could tell. But he turned away.

What she said next she felt she had to say: "If you're worried you'll have this little foreign girl chasing you around . . ." She did not have the heart to finish.

Ken nodded one of those slow, paradoxical nods that indicated disagreement. "I like you. I liked you the first time I saw you three months ago. But that's not something I'm interested in doing right now. I don't know what else to tell you, other than that you're welcome to stay. I hope you will. Your dog can even shit on my floor again. That's fine."

There was something so suddenly, stupidly tragic about him that she could not decide if she liked or despised him.

"A couple weeks ago," he said, "I did three grams of coke in a day. I got really sick after the second gram, but I didn't stop. I'm not suicidal or anything. I don't . . . I'm not sure what's happening to me."

"You're talking like an idiot again."

He sat up briskly. "How old are you?"

"Twenty-five."

"So, Maarit—how do you feel about yourself?"

She shrugged. "I don't feel anything."

"Don't hold out on me. I bet you feel terrible about yourself."

She decided she liked him, a little. "Sometimes."

"I felt that way, too, when I was twenty-five. But I look at you and I can't imagine someone in your position feeling bad about herself. You're a pretty girl, a rich girl, obviously, and you've got everything going for you." She started to say something, about her father, about her life, about her boredom and uncertainty and fears, but he plowed on: "So you feel that way, I bet, because being young is hard. Being young and smart is especially hard. And you're smart, right? Jaanus told me you went to Cambridge."

Oh, she liked him. "For a short time."

"When I was twenty-five I felt all these unfamiliar *types* of sadness. Why-do-I-have-to-die sadness. What-am-I-doing-with-my-life sadness."

"I don't feel these things. That sounds like American sadness."

"Okay, maybe, but it's also useful sadness. It's a sadness that actually makes you *do* things. In fact, I don't think it's sadness, really, at all. It's a kind of ambition that we make tolerable to ourselves by calling it sadness. The problem is that it doesn't at all prepare you for thirty-five-year-old sadness, which, as far as I can tell, has absolutely no redeeming value. What I got right now is the sadness of realizing your limitations. Worse, of *recognizing* your limitations. It's regret without having anything in particular to feel regret about. It's getting weirdly invested in matching your shower curtain to your bath mat—which I've done, by the way. It's knowing you're licked but not knowing what licked you. Oh, and get ready for all the rules to change, too. Life rules, I mean. And then you feel like a crazy person while everyone pretends the rules didn't actually change. That's been fun. I guess that's why I'm here. I figured I had a few more years of being able to live somewhere like this without being one of those people."

"Which people?"

"Those expat types. Those guys who are just sort of *around.*

All you know is that they're too old to be doing whatever it is they think they're doing."

"But you *are* one of these guys."

He looked over at her, his mouth open. It was savagely clear that this had never before occurred to him. He crumpled, a little, beside her. "I'm an asshole," he said.

Maarit's hands came down briskly on her thighs. "Look, Mr. Sadness. Either you kiss me or I leave."

"Then," he said, "I guess you leave."

For the next few days Maarit stayed in her apartment, touching with obscure disgust the many clothes in her massive walk-in closet, drinking wine from the bottle while wearing a leopard-print fur coat, walking Mimu as far as ten feet from 12 Rataskáevu's front door, and trying not to think about the strange American. She knew where he lived. Why not simply ring his bell? That was not how Maarit worked. After a few days she decided it was the cocaine she missed and texted Jaanus for a delivery. This turned out to be a cunning form of self-deception, because the moment she return-texted Jaanus she realized the only reason she wanted to see him was to ask questions about Ken. Jaanus, at any rate, did not show up; his brother Eero did. Eero had her requested two grams but apparently knew little about Ken; he'd met him only once. She did a few lines of one of the grams and then retired to her exercise room to run on her treadmill (a gift from her father). Although cocaine did not have any calories, it was still technically a carb, and Maarit was taking no chances.

After incinerating five hundred calories, Maarit, sweaty and wired and crashing with the subtlety of a 757, returned to her living room to find Mimu licking the surface of her shin-high glass coffee table. It was upon this coffee table that she had poured the portion of her gram, of which no earthly trace remained. She had been mindful enough to seal the rest of the baggie, and had not opened the other, but nevertheless left both on the coffee table. Mimu had discerned some method of ridding himself of his muzzle (it was distinctly possible she had forgotten to put it back on), after which he had licked up Maarit's poured-out coke and, apparently, eaten both baggies.

She went for her cell phone but had no idea who to call. What would cocaine do to a dog? What would it do to *Mimu*? She grabbed the first items of clothing in reach—pink T-shirt, baby-blue sweatpants, high heels—leashed Mimu (whose tongue was hanging from his mouth as though it were made of lead and whose blinkless eyes were already 90 percent pupil), and ran down the street to Ken's.

Halfway up the stairs to his apartment she heard explosions and barks and machine-gun fire. She pounded on the door over the clamor and fell weeping into Ken's arms when, at last, he opened up. Near the back of the room, on his television screen, was a great tiger-lily-orange explosion frozen in midburst. Ken was, of course, stoned. What was strange was that his neck smelled like perfume and his face like . . . yes, Maarit had gone down on enough girls to know: his face smelled unmistakably of vaginal sweat. She could not bring herself to care about that right now, even though she did, very much, and explained to him what happened. While Ken stood there, stoically thinking over the proper course of action, Mimu continued his attempt to set the world record for spinning around in circles.

They made a few quick decisions. There were three people they could not, under any circumstances, call: the police, Mimu's veterinarian, and everyone else. Maarit cried and wiped her nose while Ken poured her a glass of wine. He was certain, he said, that Mimu would be fine, so long as he voided soon. To hasten that process Ken began preparation of a bowl of grilled hamburger and olive oil. At the same time, Maarit ground up half a dozen Metamucil tablets Ken had in his medicine cabinet. Mimu was reluctant to sit still for more than a few seconds but nevertheless swallowed his medicine in three wolfish gulps, after which he urinated, squatting like a girl dog, in the middle of the room. He then spent an hour and a half bolting across Ken's apartment and back again, whimpering miserably, and unleashing several farts whose stench was incomprehensible. Finally, Mimu retreated to his chosen corner, his dark black asshole blooming as red as a wound. Maarit, despite Ken's objections, had a plate ready beneath Mimu's haunches and was incrementally amazed by the heaviness with which her beloved's leavings landed upon it. This was no mere bowel movement. It comprised three equally distinguished parts—a bowel trilogy. Ken took the plate from her and, with a gentleness as heartbreaking as it was thorough, squished Mimu's leavings between his bare fingers until he found the baggies, both of which were still sealed.

Probably Maarit would have refused Ken's advances that night no matter what, but he saved them both the trouble by not attempting any. Ken also didn't try to kiss Maarit the next time she saw him, or the next. This forced Maarit to wonder if one of the reasons she kept turning up at Ken's was to discover the half-life of his chaste inclinations. One of the iron laws of gender, she had believed, was that any two people of the opposite sex, provided with or punished by an excessive amount of private time together, will, at some point, kiss—out of curiosity, if nothing else. But Ken truly seemed to have moved beyond such things, and Maarit convinced herself she had only imagined the perfume and excreta she had smelled on him the night of Mimu's near overdose. Then she found several long hairs on Ken's pillowcases and within the bowl of his bathroom sink. He admitted, without embarrassment, that they all belonged to prostitutes. Maarit, with some alarm, noted the plural. Ken quickly explained that it was the *emotions* of intimacy he was trying to avoid, not intimacy itself. Maarit had a rough understanding of his logic there, which was also her father's logic, whereby ridding yourself of a problem meant changing the definition of the problem rather than the behavior that caused the problem in the first place. It was also cocaine logic. And she kept coming back.

Cocaine was not a sneak attack; it was a contract with the devil, signed in hell. They knew what they were doing. They did it because they had it and doing it felt better than not doing it. They did it and stayed in Ken's apartment and took turns exchanging long, go-for-broke paragraphs. Ken was very fond of the disquisition: on the superiority of American breakfast cereal, why disco was "more American" than jazz, and what he liked about being a foreigner in a small country. He had been in town for a week, for instance, when he ran into a locally famous filmmaker whose first feature had just been taken by Cannes. Soon enough he and Ken were drinking buddies, and one day the filmmaker suggested they pop over to the cottage of the nation's leading writer—the filmmaker's godmother, as it turned out—for some kvass and *verivorst*. Ken was astonished to discover that the nation's leading writer, a woman frequently on the Nobel short list, was poor enough to live in a fireplace-heated home. And the handsome and frequently photographed young filmmaker himself worked part-time in a law office! Being a small-country celebrity, Ken said in wonderment, had no benefit *other* than celebrity. That Maarit personally knew half the people who regularly appeared on television in her country only proved Ken's point.

It became important to Maarit that Ken did not regard her

as the shallow girl she often allowed herself to be, and she described to him what growing up during the death spiral of the Soviet empire had been like. This would give her depth, she hoped. The problem was that she had few connectable memories of those years. Her sisters, on the other hand, remembered everything. Maarit suspected this was why they had graduated from the Sorbonne and Oxford while she had been unable to get through six months at Cambridge. (Ken thus became the first person to whom Maarit had ever admitted this.) She described her childhood home, which was on the coast, and then only because her father, a party member, had special permission to live there. She described walking up and down its empty beachfront and wondering, in an idle way, what the ocean beyond it contained. She described the Soviet soldiers and dogs that patrolled those beaches alongside her, looking for footprints leading out to the sea, and how, if any were found, the helicopters mobilized and the outboard-powered rigid-hull inflatable boats took to the waves. She described how her sisters used to gather the Finnish garbage that washed up along the beach—the glass Coca-Cola bottles, the plastic bags from Helsinki department stores—and secretly sold what they found to families around the Old Town. Maarit's sisters made as much money in a week selling Finnish garbage as some adults made in half a year. And Ken, to her astonishment, listened. No one here cared about these things, because such misery was shared, and shared misery was not interesting, especially the misery of those, like Maarit, whose misery was so qualified.

One night, the first cold night of the fall, she told him that she thought her problem was that she was born at the wrong time. She was seven when her country declared its independence: old enough to know what she could have feared but young enough never to have really feared it. And now, because her father was so rich, she would never have to be afraid of anything. It was like there was no point in her being alive. No struggle. No worry. Nothing to endure or overcome. If she never existed, would it even matter? Ken, lying next to her in the dark, said of course her existence mattered. Maarit then closed her eyes and tried to sleep and may have, but was roused by the sound of him rolling over toward the bedside table and snorting several lines from the little mirror that, weeks ago, she had bought for him. Across the room her phone buzzed with an incoming text. She was pretty sure who it was.

Earlier that night, Maarit had gone on a date with a Finnish DJ. He had taken her to Le Bonaparte, the nicest restaurant in the Old Town. After the date, she fucked him in her apartment (she had to lock Mimu in her exercise room, where he remained) and immediately afterward demanded the Finn leave. He did so in Finnish fashion, which is to say without meaningful comment. She had then walked black-heartedly to Ken's apartment. The Finn was probably now texting her something mildly angry. She had no idea what time it was, because Ken did not have a clock in his bedroom and kept all the curtains drawn. It was probably morning. Everything cocaine did not make unbearably clear it erased.

"Isn't this nice?" Ken asked suddenly. "I really like hanging out with you like this."

"The more time I spend with you the more nice and painful feel like the same thing."

He was on his back, his hands folded on his stomach. "You can always leave. I don't want it to be painful."

"I hate you."

"Then why are you smiling?"

"How do you know I'm smiling?"

"I can hear it in your voice."

"I'm smiling because you're an idiot."

"You keep saying that."

"I had sex with a Finnish man a few hours ago."

He was quiet for a moment. "Wow."

She flung her arm over him and pressed her face into his chest. "I don't believe you don't care."

"I'm morbidly curious. Beyond that, I don't have anything to say."

"Tell me. Who is the last person you loved? What woman did this to you?"

"Maarit." His voice, suddenly, was cold.

Without really meaning to, Maarit started to cry, quietly, in the dark. She could hear his heart's hoofbeat beneath her ear.

"Okay," he said, after she sniffled. "What if I told you it was someone who died?"

Maarit ran a few brisk calculations. Then she said, "I would say you're lying."

Ken, she guessed, ran his own calculations. Then: "You'd be right. That's a lie. I could tell you something else, though. Something that wouldn't be a lie."

"And what's that?"

"I hurt her, and she hurt me. It's a boring story. And a story I have no wish to relive. What I like about you and this is that you can't hurt me and I can't hurt you."

She rose up and started hitting him, playfully, on the shoulder, and then, as the hitting went on, not so playfully, and suddenly he was holding her arms down and on top of her and staring her in the face. Her legs instinctively scissored around him, and for a few seconds he grinded against her. Something fissiony began happening between Maarit's legs. Then Ken realized what he was doing, what he was starting, stopped grinding, released her, and rolled over and sat on the bed's edge, his head lowered. "Let's go for a walk," he said.

"It's cold outside," she said.

"Yeah. That's pretty much the idea."

When they left Ken's apartment it was only half past five—not nearly as late as she feared. Unfortunately, it was twice as cold as she feared. They walked close together, his arm around her. The sky was dark but for a band of lavender along the horizon, which looked so enchantedly pretty they decided to climb to the top of Toompea, a giant limestone hill in the middle of the Old Town, where most of the rulers of her country had historically erected their ramparted headquarters, from which they gazed down in pity at sea-level life. Maarit tried to know as little as possible about the history of her hometown, but she liked walking around Toompea. She came up here so rarely it did not feel like a part of the Old Town at all.

One of the odd things about a fifteen-hundred-year-old city officially recognized as a World Heritage Site by the United Nations was that no one could knock any building down. Older structures either had to be renovated completely or allowed the dignity of falling down on their own. Since the economic crisis and the collapse of the construction industry, most of the local property owners were placing their faith in the latter process. Consequently, the affluence of Toompea had become atmospherically incoherent. The Parliament was up here, as were many ambassadors' residences, as was a giant Russian Orthodox church Maarit silently cursed every time she looked at it, but so were a number of seventeenth- and eighteenth-century houses with boarded-up windows and outer walls that shed great plaster continents if you as much as breathed on them. Ken wanted to break into one such ramshackle building and see what was inside, but Maarit pointed out to him the silent-alarm wire around its paintless, crumbling doorjamb.

"That makes no sense," Ken said. He looked across the street. "Though it makes more sense than *that*." A bright gold plate above one building's door was inscribed, in French and English: RESIDENCE OF THE FRENCH AMBASSADOR. He shook his head. "Makes the kidnapper's job a lot easier, doesn't it?"

"Who would kidnap the French ambassador?"

"I don't know. Muslims."

"We don't have any Muslims. We're the only capital in Europe without a mosque."

"Everyone has Muslims."

"Okay. We have a few. But I know we have no mosque."

Ken seemed frustrated he was not aware of this fact. "How do you know that?"

"I had an Arab boyfriend once. From Dubai."

"Egad."

"He complained about the lack of a mosque. But he was a nice man. He actually kissed me. Unlike you."

They walked to one of Toompea's many observation points that allowed views of the Old Town and the Baltic Sea beyond. From this angle much of the Old Town looked like one continuous imbricate red roof out of which thrust the occasional Gothic church spire. They watched the sun grow redly aloft, the streetlights turn off, the early-morning white passenger ships moving out of port and toward Helsinki like great floating icebergs strung with Christmas lights.

"I love it here," Ken said, leaning forward against the observation point's low stone wall. "Look at that. What a beautiful place. I don't think I ever want to leave."

Ken said a lot of stupid things, but at this particular stupid thing Maarit found herself getting angry. She had never met anyone so determined to misunderstand everything around him. She wondered if she was not a person in Ken's mind but a character in some story he would not even bother to write. She had stories, too, that she would never write, but she was not so careless with them. She thought about the life she had once imagined for herself. Leaving her small country, discovering another, marrying an Englishman, forgetting all the small-country people and rules and strictures, all the small-country problems and limitations and vacancies. The place in which you are born condemns you to one mystery. For most people that is enough. But she wanted another mystery. And this stupid American with his stupid ideas and stupid compulsions believed he had figured out another mystery, her mystery, and he understood her so little that he did not even think to keep this to himself. Had he listened to her at all?

"You don't belong here," Maarit said, still caring for him enough to allow him a way to apologize to her.

He stared out onto the Old Town, his hands flat on the wall's ledge. "And that's *exactly* what I like about it."

"Then you're a stupid man." She started to walk away.

He did not, however, come after her, as she hoped he would. So she turned. He was still standing by the wall, smiling in a cautious, unhappy way. He asked, "What is it?"

"How long before I come to knock on your door and find you dead on your couch? You can't stay in a place you don't belong."

At this he threw up his hands. Then, emboldened, he climbed onto the low stone wall and gracelessly twirled around, his arms out. Maarit was looking at his feet, which had less than half a meter to maneuver on either side. "Look at me," he said. "Do I look like I don't belong?"

In her chest some kind of mild cardiac event was under way. But she kept her bearing and voice as even as possible. "Right now you look like you're near to hurting yourself."

Ken turned to face the Old Town. His arms were lowered. The pale blue dawn sky beyond him was streaked with bright cold colors—sapphire, garnet—that she had heard many visitors claim were unique to Baltic mornings. Ken looked back at her, over his shoulder, and made a great theatrical gesture of taking a step off the wall.

She took a single pace forward. "Ken—"

"I told you," he started to say, but his foot lowered onto nothing and he pitched forward and disappeared.

Insofar as anyone who falls off a high ledge and breaks both of his legs could be considered lucky, Ken was lucky. He struck an underhanging porch beneath the larger, upper observation point, which altered his trajectory enough to allow him to land on the roof of a small building thirty, rather than eighty, feet below the ledge. By the time Maarit was able to get to him, Ken had ingested the cocaine he had left over by rubbing it against his gums, after which he tossed the packet. Maarit rode with him in the ambulance, claiming to the paramedics that she was his girlfriend. She was not, obviously, and now knew she never would be. Maarit had one big question for Ken, and it could not wait. "Why did you make me watch that?"

Ken was complicatedly strapped to his stretcher. His neck was in a brace. She discerned the tremendous pain he was in from how little he blinked; it was as though he were riveted by his own agony. Ken swallowed and said, "I sort of believed I wouldn't fall."

"Once again," she said, "you are an idiot."

"I know I am. And I think I broke a lot of things."

"Try not to move."

" 'There is no try.' Yoda."

She lifted his hand to her mouth to kiss it, but did not. Holding it felt like enough.

"I have to tell you something," he said, his eyes meeting hers for the first time since she sat beside him. "Jaanus showed me some naked pictures of you once."

She knew the photos of which Ken spoke. They were taken by Jaanus, with an iPhone camera, at his apartment, a year ago, when she was too fucked up to care. Jaanus had promised her that he deleted them. Maarit was intrigued by how little Ken's revelation bothered her at this moment.

"It was," Ken said, "a really dickish thing to do. That said, they were phenomenal pictures."

"When did this happen?"

"Way, way before I knew you. Months and months ago."

"Why are you telling me this now?"

"Because you're my friend and I care about you."

"Okay." She was embarrassed by, and possibly did not trust, the degree to which Ken's confession touched her. "And you're my friend. My stupid, stupid friend."

He broke eye contact and swallowed again. "That sounds like a pretty good thing to be."

"But I already have friends. Many friends. Why do I need another friend?"

"Where have your friends been lately?"

"I've been a bad friend to them. Also they're not as helpless as you. Remember, this is a small country."

"Let's be friends because we understand each other."

"Right now I cannot agree with you."

"But let's still be really, really good friends."

She kissed him on the forehead. "And that's all you'll get from me, friend."

He closed his eyes but immediately opened them again. "Is it just me, or do the ambulance sirens sound weird here? They sound more like police sirens."

Maarit said she did not know anything about that and pressed Ken's hand against her chest. She did not notice the nearby paramedic, who was looking at her and Ken in an expressionless yet, still, a plainly judgmental way—the look of a man, Maarit might have thought, had she noticed him, who was asked to show up too late too often and deal with problems he had no need to understand.

The Fifth Category

John woke up somewhere over the Atlantic Ocean. Oddly, though, he did not remember falling asleep or even wanting to fall asleep. He didn't sleep on planes, ever. He worked. His last memory: drinking a Diet Coke, chatting with his neighbor, Janika, a tall Estonian woman with a mischievous wood-sprite face, who told John she was on her way to the United States for her first visit. John certainly did not remember pulling the blanket up to his chin or inserting behind his head the wondrously soft pillow he now felt there. And he would have remembered. A bedtime habit of his, dating from childhood, was putting a memory lock on his sleeping position—the spoon, the scissor, the dead man, the fetus, the sprawl—just before the final fade. Only twice in his life had he found himself in the same position upon waking. For John, sleep was a kind of time travel. Things happened, thoughts formed, body parts moved—and you would never know.

Janika was gone. She'd probably opted for a stretch. Europeans and their ridiculous in-flight calisthenics, their fatuous applause on landing. The cabin's every lozenge window shade had been pulled down. The only illumination was provided by the glowing orange ellipses of the cabin's running lights. John lifted his window shade. What he saw could not be. His flight landed in New York at 4:00 p.m. It was not a night flight. And yet, outside: endless night. Janika's seat, John now realized, was not the only vacant one. The remaining forty-odd business-class seats were also empty. He lunged for his seat belt.

The cozily paired thrones of business class were spread spaciously throughout the cabin and no overhead luggage compartments hindered his movement around them. Many were draped with twisty blankets. Others had headphones still plugged into their armrest jacks. Half a dozen pillows littered the floor. Carryons remained stuffed under a number of seats. One aisle over someone had left the seat tray extended, and on it sat a perfume-sized bottle of red wine and a plastic glass. Above every seat hovered an aura of abrupt abandonment.

Something happened, he guessed, that gathered everyone's attention back in coach. A drunken Finn punching out a flight attendant. Maybe a heart attack. John whipped aside the thin blue curtain that allowed those in coach to merely imagine their deprivation. His hand quickly sought the steadying reality of the gray partition from which the curtain hung.

Before him spanned thirty darkened rows of unfilled seats. Out of shock he took a single step forward. He reached for his iPhone, sensing its absence before his hand touched his pocket. Despite the darkness, he saw a few crude shapes on the first row of the seats: paperbacks, newspapers, a briefcase. It grew darker the deeper into the rows he walked, as though he were entering a synthetic jungle.

How fundamentally wrong it felt to run down the narrow aisle of a commercial aircraft. When he reached the tight dark aft quarters he felt trapped in a bewildering, unfamiliar closet. His hands fumbled for the braille of the visible world. The attendants' jump seats were up. Adjacent to one of them was a mounted flashlight, which he pulled from its cradle. He slashed a blade of light across the kitchen, its long silver drawers looking like they belonged in a submarine, and over an unloaded dinner cart pushed back into the kitchen's deepest recess. He turned, the light passing an overhead container marked FIRST AID, and brought the beam to bear upon one of the plane's exit doors—an immense thing, less like a door than an igloo's facade. Out of its tiny porthole window John saw layers of wing-sliced cloud swirling in the starless night. He turned to the attendants' control panel, complicated by numerous knobs and buttons. Even though it was a Finnair flight, everything was in English. At the bottom of the panel was a red evac button. He worked his way up past several call buttons (all dark), a small green screen glowing with utterly unfathomable information, a public announcement button, and finally the lighting panel, which held not buttons but knobs, all of which he began turning.

In the harsh new light he opened the door to the lavatory, half expecting to find a magically immense room in which several hundred people were waiting with pointy party hats and confetti. But it was empty, shockingly white, and smelled of shit and spearmint. Transparent blisters of standing water adorned the sink's metal basin.

He charged back up coach, through business class, and found himself at the cockpit door, which had a thick, reinforced look: *hardened* was the technical term. How to proceed was unclear. Any display of forcefulness so close to the pilots seemed to John both unwise and potentially unlawful. So he knocked. When no one answered he attempted to open it. Locked. He knocked yet again. He noticed a small, knee-level cabinet. Inside were four yellow life jackets and some kind of heavy steel air compressor. He looked at the fore's exit door, another glacial immensity. He was not sure he could figure out how to open it if he tried. But why would he want to? John realized he was already considering a thirty-five-thousand-foot free fall as a potentially viable exit plan. That did not bode well.

He was sweating now. His body, as though having at last accepted, analyzed, and rejected the information his mind had sent forth, began its pointless counterattack. From his stomach, the staging area, his body spit his most recent meal into his intestinal coils. He stood there, clenched, listening to his heart pump, his lungs fill and empty. His nervous system seemed a single concentration lapse from going offline.

He pounded on the cockpit door, shouting to whomever was inside that something had happened, he needed help. When, finally, he stopped, his forehead came to rest against the door's reinforced outer shell. He felt weak and white-bellied and exposed. He then heard something on the door's other side and jumped back, not yet willing to believe he had heard it. Slowly, he closed back in, fitting his ear within the cup his hand formed against the cold metal. On the other side of this door, in the cockpit of a plane with no passengers, someone was weeping.

He had been advised not to travel outside the United States by his lawyer, his sympathetic university colleagues (he had more than most would have guessed—John was nothing if not the soul of faculty-meeting affability), and those few from Justice to whom he still spoke. But when an invitation to speak at a conference (International Law and the Future of American-European Relations) in Tallinn, Estonia, was first extended six months ago, John did what he always did: he talked to his wife.

One of the things he appreciated most about leaving government service was that he could, once again, talk to his wife about his work. For the last two years she had been his confidante, sentinel, nurse, and ballast. It was, nevertheless, one of his marriage's longer, more difficult nights when a number of the memos he'd written at Justice were leaked and then, without any warning to him, declassified and disavowed. Yet his wife was not the only person to whom he had proved capable of clarifying his intentions when he wrote those memos. Most of the journalists who actually took the time to come see John came away admitting that the purported werewolf behind the so-called torture memos seemed a decent enough fellow.

Two years ago, a complaint accusing John of war crimes had been filed in a German court. Another suit was filed six months ago, in a California court, by a convicted American terrorist and his mother, who claimed John's memos had led to his maltreatment while in U.S. custody. John did not dispute, though of course could not admit, that the wretch had been treated poorly in custody, but drawing the line back to him evidenced a kind of naive legal creationism. While John's travel was by no means formally restricted, the thought of leaving American airspace filled him with apprehension.

Thus, after telling his wife about the conference invitation, he was surprised to find himself admitting, "My first thought was to say no. But I think I want to go."

"Don't route your flight through Germany," his wife said. "Or France. Or Spain. I'd avoid Italy, too, for that matter."

Obviously, she thought he was joking about going abroad to speak, so he waited a moment before telling her what he liked about Estonia, a young country with memories of actual oppression. He had always been interested in the nations of the former Soviet bloc and postcommunist countries in general. (His grandparents' flight from Korean communism was, after all, the reason he was an American.) He did not think he had any cause to fear Estonia, which was an official American ally in the war. Was his wife aware that there were only 1.5 million Estonians in the world? Maybe it was a Korean thing, but he felt a strange kinship with small, pushed-around, frequently invaded nations.

Of course, he was now shamelessly appealing to his wife's own complicated feelings concerning her Vietnamese heritage.

She asked how he could be certain it was not simply a trap to publicly humiliate him. To that he already had something of an answer. The event's organizers had promised, unprompted, that no topics would be discussed beyond John's willingness to discuss them. They were aware of the lawsuits and promised him full escape-pod capability during any line of questioning. ("Escape pod." His words, not theirs. Like any nerd who grew up in the 1970s, John was always good for a *Star Wars* reference.) The U.S. embassy, moreover, was "aware of" John's invitation. ("Aware of." Their words, not his. A middling embassy like Estonia's was no doubt heavily staffed with administration flunkies and professional vacationists. Given that John was the only former member of the administration who insisted on talking about the decisions he had made while part of it, he was as popular among them as a leper bell.)

"But you'll talk about it all anyway," she said, "won't you?" John often reduced his lawyer to similar frustration. He was not afraid to defend himself, provided his interlocutor was not obviously carrying a torch and kindling. After John granted an interview to *Esquire* his lawyer didn't speak to him for a week. Then his lawyer read the not entirely unflattering profile that resulted. "You're a smooth one, Counsel," he told John.

John smiled at his wife. *Of course* he would talk about it all. He knew what he could and could not say. He was a *lawyer*.

When he told the event's organizers he would be coming, they expressed as much surprise as excitement. He would be the only American, they said, and as such an invaluable part of the discussion. It was agreed he would speak alone, at the close of the conference, for an hour and then answer questions, some of which, they warned, might be hostile. "Sounds fine,"

John emailed back. He had faced more bloodthirsty rooms than he imagined Estonia could muster. Before agreeing, he checked in with the embassy in Tallinn. The staffers acknowledged the conference and wished him a successful trip. The last he would hear from them, he suspected.

Six months later, he spent two hours laid over in Helsinki's airport. When two Finnish security guards stopped near John's gate to chat, he was not sure why he felt so nervous. But what man could truly relax knowing that courts on two continents had entertained the possibility he'd committed crimes against humanity? He supposed he was brave for being here. No, actually. This thought disgusted him. He was a teacher and a lawyer, in that order. He did not recall the last time he raised his voice. He did not recall once, in his four decades, having intentionally hurt anyone. The Finnish guards walked away.

He boarded the flight to Tallinn with reenergized anonymity. By the time he saw his spired, red-roofed, seaside destination appear outside the starboard window, he knew he'd made the right choice. It was noon by the time he reached his hotel in Tallinn's Old Town. Check-in was surreally pleasant. The conference's organizers had sent flowers. He called them to ask for directions to that night's conference hall, which, as it happened, was less than three blocks away, in another hotel, the Viru. No, no thank you, he could make his way there on his own. His talk was scheduled for 8:00 p.m. This meant he had the afternoon to spend in Tallinn. He did so by sleeping off the circadian catastrophe of shooting across ten time zones.

By 5:00, he was awake, showered, dressed in a cement-colored suit with a blue shirt (no tie), and wandering Tallinn's Old Town in search of dinner. The organizers had offered to send someone over to take him to dinner, but no. He wanted to announce his conference presence with the same powerful abruptness he used to enter his classrooms. If any of the conference's participants were indeed seeking to confront him, the less time they had the better.

The charms of Tallinn's Old Town were myriad and entirely preposterous. No actual human beings could live here. It looked like a soundstage for some elvish epic. The streets—the most furiously cobbled he had ever seen—appeared to shed their names at every intersection. Most took him past pubs, restaurants, shops selling amber, and nothing else. It was easy to distinguish the tourists from the locals: everyone not working was a tourist. Outside a medieval restaurant off the town square young Estonians dressed like the maidens and squires of the Hanseatic League watched as their coworkers reenacted a swordfight. On one block-long side street a blast of methane wind took hold of him: the sewage coursing through three-hundred-year-old plumbing was one bit of Tallinn's past in no need of studied re-creation. The similarity of the Old Town's many ornate black church spires confused him. Every time he settled on one as his compass back toward the Viru, he realized it was the wrong tower. For two hours he was always at least slightly lost.

From its height and brutalist design he correctly surmised that the Viru had once been the Intourist Hotel during the Soviet era. In its lobby he found a wall of fame listing some of the hotel's notable guests: Olympians, musicians, actors, Arab princes, and President Bush himself. A framed note from the president, written to the hotel manager on White House letterhead, concluded: "Thanks also for the good-looking sweater and hat." After inquiries at the front desk, an elevator ride to the conference floor, and an olfactory napalming courtesy of the perfumed woman riding up with him, John walked down a lushly carpeted hallway toward the registration desk. The young man sitting there pointed down the hall, toward a small group of people politely waiting outside the conference room proper for the current speaker to finish. John was on in half an hour. He joined the waiting listeners outside the conference room, a golden and chandeliered cavern.

The speaker was German. From the translation projected onto a screen behind the woman (in French, Estonian, and English—he, too, had been asked to send the text of his talk beforehand to the organizers, after extracting from them a promise that native English speakers would translate it) John knew he was in for a slightly rougher night than he'd been anticipating. Of course, he'd heard all the tropes of the German woman's talk before. She finished to applause and answered a few questions, after which a ten-minute break was announced. As people rose from their seats, another woman near the back of the room turned, spotted John, and, with a smile of acknowledgment, walked toward him. John met her halfway, maneuvering through the human cross-stream of intermission.

This was Ilvi Armastus, one of the organizers, his contact, and a professor of law at the University of Tartu. A very *young* professor of law, which warmed the still-youthful-looking John to her instantly. They shook, after which Ilvi began knotting her hands as though shaping a small clay ball. Pleasantries, then: flights, sleep, Tallinn. She asked, "Are you ready?" John laughed and said he thought so. She laughed, too, her enamel giving off a slight yellow tinge. Ilvi had chapped lips and a mushroom of curly brown hair. Her long and angular face was almost cubist, its unusual prettiness cohering only after you had spent some time looking at her.

For some incomprehensible reason, Ilvi guided John over to the German speaker who had just finished condemning his country. She was speaking to four people at once, all of whom stood around her. She appeared accustomed to being the center of attention; they appeared accustomed to providing attention. At

Ilvi's announcement of John's name, they all turned to consider him. He smiled, his hand thrust out. Only one person, an older man wearing a heavy wool sport coat, deigned to reach out and shake—though he did so with the dutiful air of a prisoner meeting his warden. No one said anything after that.

For far longer than John would have liked, Ilvi—whether mortified or oblivious he had no good way of surmising—stood there beside him. Finally, she escorted him to another small bundle of conference-goers, from whom he received only a few more calories of warmth. Then she led him toward the dais. He plunked down upon the lone chair and withdrew his talk from a breast pocket. Ilvi stood at the maple podium schoolmarmishly looking at her watch.

He was, by now, well inured to pariah treatment, which was not to say it didn't wound him. Sometimes students (never his; his classes were always overenrolled) wore black armbands and stood in silence on the steps outside the law school, waiting for John to pass en route to his office. A couple of times they had worn Gitmo-orange jumpsuits. He always wished them good morning. Once, and only once, he had stopped to talk to them. Their complaints were so numerous and multidisciplinary it had been like arguing with Beatnik poetry. He came away from all such experiences less befuddled than disappointed. John did not want them or anyone to agree with him. He respected considered disagreement. All he wanted was someone other than himself to admit that it was complicated.

Early in the war, two men fated to be deemed "enemy combatants" were captured in Afghanistan. One was an American citizen, the other an Australian. What laws applied to them? As John learned, you had to go very far back in the history of American jurisprudence—the Indian Wars, piracy law—to find legally appropriate analogies. Some members of the Justice Department wanted the captured American Mirandized, but every court on this planet accepted that more amorphous laws governed battle-field conduct. Treating these men as criminals meant the potential loss of what they knew. And so the American and Australian detainees did not, John argued, enjoy the protections granted to prisoners of war under Common Article III of the Geneva Conventions. Enjoying no rank, no clearly defined army, and no obvious chain of command—prerequisites upon which war-prisoner protections under Common Article III were dependent—these men could not be considered prisoners of war in any legal sense.

When the third-highest-ranking member of al-Qaeda was captured in Pakistan, John was asked to provide the CIA with legal guidance. This took much of the summer of 2002, and John could not recall having worked harder or more thoroughly on a memo. He had to determine whether interrogation techniques used by the CIA outside the United States violated American obligations under the 1984 Torture Convention. So he looked at what these obligations entailed. The first thing he learned was that torture was "any act by which severe pain or suffering, whether physical or mental, is intentionally inflicted on a person." "Severe," then, was part of the legal definition. The United States had attached to its instrument of ratification a further definition of torture as an act "specifically intended to inflict severe physical or mental pain." What was "severe pain"? What did "specifically intended" actually mean? John checked the relevant medical literature. Could a doctor define "severe pain"? A doctor could not. Did the law itself? The law did not. The fact was you could look far and wide in legal documents for a working definition of "severe pain" and never find it. So John, with no relish, provided one: in order to constitute torture, the "severe pain" must rise "to a level that would ordinarily be associated with a sufficiently serious physical condition such as death, organ failure, or serious impairment of body functions." As for "prolonged mental harm," another bit of unexplained language from the Torture Convention, it appeared nowhere in U.S. law, medical literature, or international human rights reports. Again, John had to provide his own definition. For purely mental pain or suffering to amount to torture, thus satisfying the legal requirement of "prolonged mental harm," the end result, he judged, must be akin to post-traumatic stress disorder or chronic depression of significant duration, which is to say months or years.

John had intended these guidelines to apply only to the CIA and only with regard to what were known as "high-value intelligence targets," never to common prisoners and especially not in Iraq, where Common Article III of the Geneva Conventions absolutely applied. Guantánamo was where things began to go haywire. Due to the interrogation limits the FBI agents present there were insisting upon—they wanted every bit of evidence gathered to hold up in court, forgetting (or choosing to forget) that no one in Gitmo would be tried by anything but military tribunals—a prisoner could not even be offered a Twinkie and juice box without it being deemed "coercive." Until John's memo, that is. Shortly after its guidance went into wide and, to John, unanticipated effect, the FBI's head counsel wrote his own memo that claimed the interrogations his agents were seeing at Guantánamo were illegal. The day John's memos were finally declassified, Gonzales disavowed them at a press conference, claiming they did "not reflect the policies of the administration." For this John would not forgive the attorney general, a man he once considered his friend.

The audience clapped, at least, after Ilvi's introduction, an idle plagiarism of the curriculum vitae John had sent her. He made his way to the podium, leaned toward the mic, and glanced back at the screen behind him. There it was—his talk's first block of translated text. *Okay,* he thought. *Good.*

He looked out upon the facial pointillism of his audience. Their expressions were more curious than hostile. Something then popped into his mind as suddenly as the words had appeared on the screen behind him: *This was too far to have come.* He was a tenured professor of law at a major American university. He wondered, once again, why he was so determined to defend himself. Was it so important to know that he could?

At the beginning of September 2001, John was thirty-four years old and reviewing a treaty whose most legally substantive issue involved polar bears.

Before returning to his seat John tried a couple of things. First, he hit the cockpit door with the steel air compressor approximately fifty times. Second, he returned aft, held down the PA button of the attendants' control panel, and screamed. Becoming hysterical solved nothing. Calmer now, and back in his seat, he tried to formulate a reasonable explanation for what was happening to him. He didn't think he'd been drugged. He'd eaten nothing that day and drunk only a can of Diet Coke shortly after boarding. The business-class attendant had given the can to John and he himself had opened it.

He replayed various short-term-memory fragments. The morning flight from Tallinn. Forty-five minutes in Helsinki. The bovine ordeal of boarding. He recalled as many of his fellow passengers as he could. Chatty Janika, the Estonian on her way to the United States. The neckless, bullfrogish man John had sat beside at the gate. The amply eyebrowed young woman in the Oxford sweatshirt who smiled at John as she passed by his seat on her way back to coach. (John never forgot a woman who smiled at him, unibrow or no.) A young man he recalled only because he was black. A studious, stringy-haired girl in a loose white blouse. A kid in his early twenties in a YOU SUCK T-shirt. The female flight attendants in their powder-blue pantsuits. John had been conscious of his Asianness on this Finnair flight, in this northern clime. How dearly he'd been anticipating his return to California, to his university town and its multiraciality, its music stores and eateries, its varieties of cannabis enfleurage.

But there was the matter of his iPhone. Someone had clearly taken it. He'd looked for it under his and every other seat in business class. What would he do? What *could* he do? The air compressor had done real damage to the door, denting its hardened shell and knocking off the handle. The handle was now in John's pocket, in case he needed to fix it later, though he had no idea how he might manage that. He'd found some tools in an aft storage cabinet, which were now on the seat beside him.

Almost certainly dozens of passengers aboard this plane had been carrying phones, too, any number of which might still be in their carry-ons. While getting reception on them was unlikely, he might be able to find a device that allowed the sending of a stored email or text once the plane reached a lower altitude. Before he could go find such a phone, the plane shook as though withstanding atmospheric reentry. He buckled his seat belt. His fear, having almost come under the control of his hope, felt newly feral. He breathed. He was not sure what time it was or how long he'd been on this plane, but his window shade, like every other window in business class, was now open, and once again he stared into the freezing darkness of the troposphere. He then thought of his wife, his students, and their concern for him. Yet again, he rose from his seat.

John felt strangely better once he had all the business-class carry-ons gathered around him. Remaining close to his appointed seat seemed important, though he could not explain why. He worked his way through the bags, most of which were small. People who paid business-class fares did not hesitate to check their luggage. They had no cab line to beat; they landed to find Jordanian men holding small white signs bearing their last names. Unzipping the luggage only as much as needed, John slipped his hand into one opening after another and felt and squeezed and searched. He did not want to unnecessarily disturb anyone's items. Anything that felt at all promising he pulled out through its zippered caul. By the end of his search he sat among shaving kits, digital cameras, iPods, duty-free bottles of vodka with Cyrillic lettering, several Montblanc pens, and a smooth pink plastic torpedo he had realized only incrementally was a sex toy. Also accounted for were half a dozen computer cases, every one of which was empty.

He moved on to coach, but before he'd managed to empty a single overhead container, his stomach sent another dose of fiery waste toward its point of egress. He staggered to the bathroom, unbuckled his pants, and sprayed before he could get himself atop the metal-basined toilet's plastic ring. The smell had no equivalent he could name. It was, somehow, an *orange* smell. His intestinal spigot opened yet again; waste escaped him in avid bursts. He was sick now, and dizzy, his brain an invalid no one had thought to visit in months. When he finished he washed his hands.

Decorousness no longer concerned him. He walked down the first aisle opening the overheads and savagely throwing their contents to the floor. Soon enough he was knee-deep in baggage. He wasn't yet ready to search them. His anger was too overriding now; he'd need to regenerate the care and attentiveness properly excavating these bags would require. Thus he moved on to the second aisle, pushing its overheads' release buttons as he went. After a satisfying pop the doors slowly lifted open. So much of this plane was kept in place by plastic hinges. He was inside a metal tube, sailing just beneath the fringe of outer space, while huge engines fifty feet from him spewed invisible 1,000-degree fire. Was that any less remarkable than the reality he was now trapped inside?

He found Janika in the aisle's third-to-last overhead, however unhappily she fit. Her bruised, cross-eyed face and masking-taped mouth sent John to the floor as resoundingly as a blow. When he finally looked back up at her he saw that one of her arms had slipped from its containment. Her hand vibrated lightly in turbulence he could no longer feel. He carefully removed her from the overhead. When the last of her body was pulled free she seemed to gain one hundred spontaneous pounds. Not expecting this, John fell back, with Janika on top of him, onto a bed of carry-ons and their pointily jutting contents.

Janika's crossed eyes, so close to John's own but unable to meet them, seemed troubled by some final, unwanted knowledge. Dried red crumbles of blood filled her nostrils. John pushed her away and made long, loud primate sounds. He tried pulling the masking tape from Janika's mouth, but the sound of skin tugging against dead musculature was so nightmarish he stopped and ran screaming back toward business class.

He decided to once again beat the cockpit door with the air compressor. This time, however, he decided he wouldn't stop. Yet he entered business class to find that the screen upon which the preflight PSA had been broadcast was lowering. The cabin lights then went soundlessly out. Panic spun him around. Two steps into his dash back to coach he stumbled and fell. Unable to see, he crawled along an uneven reef of luggage. What he had been feeling until now was not fear. Not really. Fear was liquid; it traveled the bloodstream; it sought the reservoir of the brain. Its power derived not from what could happen but from what you realize will happen. Above him was a sound of small, whirring industry. Throughout coach, screens were lowering into place. John looked at the closest one, the screen glowing like vinyl: darker, somehow, than actual darkness.

Then: an image of crisp digital-video quality, though its bottom edge vaguely flickered with waveform. John was too far away to make any sense of it. He stood. What he saw when he was close enough to the screen was a small plywood room, filmed from the high-corner angle unique to surveillance. Within the room were two figures. In a chair, behind a small table: a woman. Circling her: a man in boots, loose black pants, black tank top, black ski mask. The audio was tinny, far away, obviously unmic'd. In the blizzardy imperfection of poorly lit digital video, John did not immediately recognize Janika. She appeared to have been tied to her chair and was crying in a quietly hopeless way. The man looked over at the camera, walked toward it, and finally reached up and grabbed it. The camera was not fixed in some surveillance perch at all; it was a handheld. The image went whirlwind but quickly stabilized, save for a few handheld jiggles.

A second man, identically dressed, entered the room through a hitherto unnoticed door. Looking directly into the camera, he pulled the door shut behind him. The first camera-wielding man went into zoom as the second approached, for his ski-masked face now filled the screen. John stared at this man staring back at him. Now that she was blocked from sight, Janika's soft, wet sobs were sharper, more keening.

The man himself said nothing. His eyes were animate in no remarkable way. When, at last, he turned away, he busied himself at the table. Now the man was writing something, John realized, and once he finished he again faced the camera. He held out a piece of thin white cardboard filled with letters of nearly perfect contiguousness. John did not expect the sign to say what it did. He nonetheless felt grateful when he read it, for now he better understood what was happening and why. The man placed the sign on the table before fixing his attention upon Janika, who now screamed. As for the sign, John could still see it: CATEGORY I.

After his speech, Ilvi asked John if he would like to join her and some others, including the speaker who preceded him, for drinks in the Old Town. Was this woman truly that stupid? John extricated himself from her offer with an obsequious bow, a claim of exhaustion, and multiple thank-yous. He was beginning to feel both ghostly and loathed here, less a man than an unpleasant idea. As he made his way toward the exit, people scattered from his path as though he were lobbing lit firecrackers. For how much longer would this be his life?

A few of the questions he'd taken were indeed hostile, the most pointed posed by an older woman in the front row with a face as tight-skinned as a kayak. She'd demanded to know what John would do in the event of a formal accusation of war crimes by the International Criminal Court. John: "I'm not that worried about it, to be perfectly honest."

Although John had another day scheduled in Tallinn, he stepped into a men's room off the hallway outside the conference room and stabbed at his iPhone until he was online. The conference had paid for John's flight but, at his request, left the return ticket open. Within a couple of minutes that ticket was changed.

Magic. Less magical was the fact that he was now $5,500 poorer. It was hard to regard this as anything but a bargain.

John exited to find a gleamingly clean-shaven man waiting for him. His outfit was that of a tech executive, Halloween version: navy-blue sport coat, no tie, jeans, cross-trainers. Obviously American. The man's face filled with an expression of unilateral recognition that John, despite his notoriety, had still not grown used to, because this type of recognition always failed to acknowledge itself as unilateral. Instead it said to John: *I know who you are; you should therefore be happy to meet me.* Everyone was the star of his own story.

The man said John's name and extended his hand. A business card emblazoned with the embassy seal materialized. RUSSELL GALLAGHER, CULTURAL LIAISON OFFICER. In John's limited experience, words such as *cultural* and *officer* tended to serve as camouflage for intelligence work.

John tried to give the card back but Gallagher insisted that he keep it. John put it into his pocket and asked, "Are you my envoy?"

Gallagher had a boyish appearance, though age was beginning its erosive work around his eyes and along his hairline. "I'm not, unfortunately. You're not too popular at the embassy. You probably know this already but they tried to get you uninvited to this thing."

John was aware that, among the remaining loyalist vestiges of the Bush administration, he could expect no grata shown his persona. But that an embassy would attempt to block his appearance at an international conference seemed astonishing. Did these people not have anything better to do? "As a matter of fact," he told Gallagher, "I did *not* know that."

The indiscretion was cause for some light, quick laughter on Gallagher's part. "It turns out your friend Professor Armastus doesn't like to be pushed around. She also has friends. The harder the embassy lobbied the more determined they were to get you here. Great speech, by the way."

"She's hardly a friend. Tonight's the first time I met her. But thank you."

"Look," Gallagher said, his demeanor hardening, "I'm here, under my own volition, to tell you that a lot of us are grateful to you and what you did."

"Thank you again."

Gallagher looked at John for a moment. "My father was a Vietnam vet, 'seventy-one to 'seventy-two. One of the things he was involved with was the Phoenix Program. He always said it got such a bad name because it was created by geniuses and carried out by idiots. But even then it was the most effective thing we ever threw against the Viet Cong. The communists admitted as much after the war. My dad was in Saigon, and he told me that by 1972 the average life expectancy of a communist cell leader in the city was about four months. And nothing you argued for was worse than what my dad was proud to have done with Phoenix. Just wanted you to know there are a lot of us who admire you."

While drafting his memos John had actually looked into the Phoenix Program. He learned that the CIA had made internal promises that Phoenix would be "operated under the normal laws of war." He also learned that several American officers involved with Phoenix asked to be relieved of their duties because they thought that what they were doing was immoral.

John looked back at Gallagher. The man's posting in the target-poor environment of Estonia spoke for itself. His father hunted down commies. The hottest action the son could scare up for himself was defying his embassy in order to tell John to keep his chin up. The conservatism of which Gallagher was doubtless a disciple was not a proper philosophy. It was a bad mood. Neither of them said anything for several seconds.

"You want a drink?" Gallagher asked. "You look like you could use one."

They walked out of the Viru together and into the enduring 10:00 p.m. sunlight of a Tallinn summer evening. John asked Gallagher how long he'd been posted here. "I was in Greece before this. Ten years in. Before that, the Marines. Made captain in 1998. Got out too early for any of the fun stuff."

They were walking toward the center of the Old Town. In the weakening light the buildings seemed as bright as animation cells. People were drinking in the cafés along the sidewalk, drinking while they walked, drinking while they waited for ATM slots to stick out their tongues of currency. John noted the packs of young Russian men with hard eyes and unsteady gaits, the singing arm-entwined Scotsmen, the wobbling smokers standing outside every pub. He also noticed the tiny old begging women dressed in seasonally inappropriate clothing, every one of them looking like victims of some unbreakable hex. John asked Gallagher, "With what sort of culture do you typically liaise around here?"

Gallagher chuckled. "You might be surprised. But it's a fun place to live, even if Estonians are sort of inscrutable. A buddy of mine plays bass, and he told me that wherever he's lived in the world he's always been able to show up at open mics. Everyone needs a bass player. When he got to Tallinn he'd show up at an open mic and there'd be five Estonian guys standing there with their basses, looking for a lead guitarist. This is a nation of bass players."

John's eyes snagged on two high-heeled Freyas in dermally tight jeans walking toward him. In their wake they left all manner of shouted Russian entreaties.

Gallagher noticed the women, too. "And, of course, there's that. In Tallinn even the ugly girls are kind of pretty. This is off-set by the fact that even the intelligent ones are kind of stupid."

Gallagher went on as they walked. Talk of women became talk of Finland, which became talk of the Soviet special forces, which became a condensed narrative history of the 1990s. Segues were nonexistent. Soon the soliloquy returned to his father. John was no longer listening. Instead he considered Gallagher. His hair was thin, limp, the color of rye, and Gallagher was often pet-ting it forward to conceal his retreating hairline. Discussing his father left Gallagher wallowing in unspecified grievances, though he still insisted on laughing every third or fourth sentence. "And that's what my dad always said," Gallagher concluded.

John, having failed to catch the gist of Gallagher's finale (there may not have been one), nodded.

Gallagher did, too. Then: "He died last year."

"I'm sorry for your loss."

"When your memos were leaked we even talked about it. I asked him for his opinion. He predicted that the terrorists were going to use our own courts against us. He said, 'Shit, I per-sonally violated Article III of the Geneva Conventions. Several times!'"

Gentle crinkles of preoccupation formed across John's brow. This drink was a mistake.

"Here we go." Gallagher was pointing to a belowground bar just off Pikk, an absurdly pretty street John had wandered up and down earlier that day. Christmas lights were strung up in its basement windows; there was no sign. John did not drink, at least not in any way that conceptually honored what people meant by "drinking": a glass of wine every few nights, always with a meal; an occasional imported beer on hot Sunday afternoons. When

Gallagher mentioned a drink, John imagined the two of them sharing a tumbler of cognac in a wine bar.

John followed Gallagher down concrete bomb-shelter stairs. Already uncomfortable, he became more so when Gallagher pushed open the door and instantly repaired to the bar—a hale fellow, well met—where he had words with the gorgeous apparition toiling behind it. John decided to play a little game with himself to see how long he could last here. He found a table and waited for Gallagher to join him, but when he looked back Gallagher was holding the bartender's hand. He then turned it over and traced out with his index finger some elaborate fortune-teller augury on her palm. Smiling, the bartender pulled her hand free and worked the tap while Gallagher looked smugly around. She air-kissed him while handing over his requested two pints. Gallagher raised the glasses in thanks. The moment his back was to her the woman stopped smiling.

As for the bar's other patrons: there did not appear to be any. John had chosen as his landing site the most centrally located of the room's four tables. Sparsely arranged along one wall's tragically upholstered booth were half a dozen cross-armed young women staring at the ceiling, their purses in their laps. At the other end of the room another woman danced on a stage no larger than the table at which John now sat. Thankfully, she was not stripping, and did not appear to be interested in stripping, but rather moved in a languidly bored way to music so timidly broadcast that John could barely hear it. The walls and carpet were inferno red, making hellishness the bar's only recognizable motif. Gallagher planted himself in the chair across from John and pushed a beer toward him. "It doesn't usually get hopping here till one or two."

John motioned around. "What is this?"

In mid-sip, Gallagher's eyebrows lifted. When he lowered the glass his tongue agilely shaved off his froth mustache. "A place for discerning gentlemen. Don't worry. It's nothing you don't want it to be."

With that the dancing woman, sweaty and luminous, came and sat next to John. She was wearing a black dress that could have fit inside a coin purse. John looked plaintively at his host. "Gallagher, please."

Gallagher laughed again. "One drink, Counsel. It's a nice place to relax if you let yourself." To the dancing woman he then said, "Sweetheart, *davai*. Come sit next to me." She did. The next woman who came over Gallagher tried to wave off, but she sat next to John anyway.

John shook her hand. Her legs were ruinously thin, her stretch pants tight around her thighs but barely holding shape against her calves. She studied her foot as she tapped it against the red carpeting, which looked as though it had been the recipient of many gastric sorrows. Her toenails were the unreal color of aluminum foil. John still said nothing to her. Gallagher, meanwhile, was getting along well with the dancing woman. Honestly. It appeared they were having a fairly serious conversation.

The woman next to John lit a cigarette and took one of those long, crackling drags that actually made cigarettes seem appealing. Secondhand smoke leaked from the corners of her mouth. After another minute of this, she left, and John was alone with his beer.

What no one asked John after his speech was whether he suffered any reservations while writing his memos. John did have occasional reservations. They all did. Part of him wished he'd had a chance to talk about that. For instance, John's biggest worry was that interrogators might not feel restrained by the same moral qualms that, say, a middle-aged lawyer would. He also worried about what was called "force drift," where force applied unsuccessfully has no choice but to become force applied again, but more intently. After all, enhanced interrogation was excusable only if the person being interrogated was presumed to know something. This was why he never imagined it being applied to anyone but confirmed al-Qaeda members.

John understood his arguments were controversial and sometimes even repellent, but they were legal rather than moral judgments. John did not craft policy or devise what form "enhanced interrogation" actually took. He simply measured legality against relevant statutes. His memos had been concerned with eighteen methods, which came in three categories. The first category was limited to two techniques: yelling and deception. The second category comprised twelve: stress positions, isolation, forced standing for up to four hours, phobia exploitation, false documents, removal from standard interrogation sites, twenty-four-hour-long interrogations, food variation, removal of clothing, forced grooming, deprivation of light, and loud music. The third category, intended for use only against the hardest cases, broke down into four techniques: mild physical contact (slapping, pushing), scenarios that threatened the death of the detainee or his family, extreme element exposure, and simulated drowning. There was also a fourth category, which, thankfully, he had never been asked to rule on. The fourth category was also the loneliest. Its one technique: extraordinary rendition, wherein interrogation was outsourced to allied nations whose prisons were unburdened by legal regulation. We pretended not to know they tortured, they pretended not to torture, and our magically pliant prisoners were delivered back to us.

John had told himself, while contemplating leaving Justice,

that it would be better outside. Walks across an autumn quad, adoring students waiting outside his office, the intramural atmosphere Washington could never provide except in venal approximation. Justice was a museum and its cold marble hallways led to a kind of intellectual progeria. How quickly even the young there became old. Addington was the saddest to see John go. *Do you really,* Addington asked, *want to teach spoiled rich kids who give murdering proletarian mobs a good name?*

Within months of John's departure, many of his judgments were withdrawn and then suspended. John later learned that Addington protested this by saying the president had been relying on John's views. In that case, the answer came back, the president may have been breaking the law. Five months later, Abu Ghraib. Seven months later, John's memos were declassified. Gonzales, at the press conference, claimed to want to show the media that due diligence and proper legal vetting had occurred at every step in the enhanced interrogation process. That was what he actually believed was at issue.

John would never forget the rattlesnake energy coiled in those war council meetings. They were all as confident as Maoists. Feith, Haynes, Addington, Gonzales, Flanigan—men one step away from the president. The lawyer's lawyers. The nation had suffered a heart attack and they were holding the paddles of defibrillation, working together to improvise legal strategies for something no law as yet existed to contain. They met in Gonzales's office in the White House, sometimes at Defense. Simple, uncatered, unrecorded meetings in which the most luxurious staples were a few Diet Cokes. John often looked at himself and Gonzales during these meetings. John was a first-generation American, Gonzales the son of immigrants so impoverished they did not have a telephone. And yet here they were, drafting policy during the most serious national security crisis in half a century, serving as personal counsel to the world's most powerful man. This was the America that made John willing to do anything legal to protect it.

Then you had Feith and Addington, androids who regarded other human beings as collections of mental malfunctions. The dimples within Feith's rumpled Muppet face were venom repositories. He circulated memos without buck slips so no one could be sure to whom they were routed or cc'd people who never actually received them. He made speeches on the sanctity of Geneva only to heighten the incongruity of its sacred shroud being filthied by terrorists. His was such manifestly confusing lawyering that those who heard Feith talk about Geneva came away believing Article III *would* apply to everyone the United States captured. By the end of one of Feith's monologues he had one of the Joint Chiefs mistakenly believing that all eighteen enhanced interrogation techniques were sanctioned by the Army Field Manual. Not one of them actually was. The idea to launch a new intelligence agency called Total Information Awareness, the logo of which was a crazy Masonic eye overlooking the world? Only Feith.

As for Addington: the eyes of a Russian icon, the bearing of Lincoln, the disposition of a hand grenade. After the attacks Addington began carrying a copy of the Constitution in his pocket so worn and flimsy it looked like it had served as a hankie or coaster or both. Whenever anyone disagreed with him, he would pull it out and start reading from it. It was Addington's special genius to frame every legal and moral argument in warlike terms, whereas any argument about actual warfare came draped in diaphanous euphemism. Maybe that was why, out of all of them, only Addington had escaped. Only he had managed to keep his name off every relevant document.

Three people had been subjected to the waterboarding.

Three people. And for that he had to answer questions about war crimes? John later heard that his successor allowed himself to be waterboarded before supplying a decision about whether it was over the line. The answer: It was. But for all that, for all the debate and decapitated careers, the CIA was still allowed to use simulated drowning (John actually preferred this more honest term over *waterboarding*), just as John had originally argued. His core arguments were still in place. Of course, no one in Justice wanted to sign off on the CIA's use of the technique, but the president found his man. He always did. But that was bitterness, and John was not bitter. He would have liked to see Feith or Gonzales or Ashcroft or any of them, alone in a European city, answering questions about policies they had endorsed but were presently ashamed of.

John looked down into his pint glass, now an empty crystal well. Somehow he had drunk his beer. He could brood here, he knew, all night and let the dark wave carry him.

"I'm ready to leave," he told Gallagher, who was still having his edifying conversation with the dancer.

He looked over at John. "I hope you made time to see the Museum of Occupations tomorrow."

"I can't, actually. I'm leaving in the morning." John looked at his watch. It was already past midnight.

Gallagher sat back. "A shame. Tallinn's a nice place to spend a day in."

"Thank you for the drink," John said, standing. "Feel free to stay. I can find my way back."

Gallagher remained seated but extended his hand. "I hope someday we might meet again. Have a good flight tomorrow."

At the door, John turned around for one last glimpse of Gallagher. He was on his cell, bent over in his chair, the dancer getting up to leave. Gallagher noticed John lingering in the doorway and shot him a not-very-sharp salute. Hard to believe that guy was a Marine. John wondered, though only for a moment, to whom Gallagher might be speaking.

Janika's interrogation film had been over for twenty minutes or an hour. It was impossible to keep track of time in the darkness. Light gave time's passage handholds and markers. Time passed in the dark was like driving through cornfields—an endless similarity, filled with the unseen.

What the film was intended to provoke in him he did not know. He was no more or less sympathetic to those he had helped doom to torture than he was before the film began. They misunderstood him. They did not comprehend what he had actually argued for. Those in command of this plane and, now, his life had nothing to gain from him, other than invigorating their sadism. He, in return, had nothing he could give them, other than the gift of his torment. Torture, he had written, was a matter of intent. He now knew that torture was many more things than that.

Suddenly John was staring at the plane's ceiling, its vaguely surgical nozzles gushing air. Yes, the lights were back on. He wrenched around in his adopted coach seat and was not quite prepared to see Janika's broken body, still tangled in luggage, near the aft. When he stood, gusts of sickness-spiced air were pushed through the cloth chimneys of his clothing.

In the film, Janika's tormentor had moved through Category I and the more visually operatic techniques of Categories II and III, at which point several other men had entered the room. What happened next was as dreadful as anything John had seen. He refused to watch most of it and opened his eyes only after the sounds of her struggle had ceased. While the men were verifying the extinguishment of Janika's vital signs, the film had stopped.

John returned to his designated seat. Upon it sat his iPhone, as white as a wafer. A dumb flood of thought branched off toward what few remaining lowlands it could. One of them was Gallagher, the only person who knew that John had changed his flight. Gallagher's card was still in his breast pocket. He took it out and looked at it, his thumb playing over the raised embassy seal. He wondered how Gallagher knew he would not throw the card away. He wondered how it could be that Janika was wearing the same clothes in the interrogation video as she had been when John met her. He wondered how long he had actually been unconscious and whether this was even the plane he'd boarded. He wondered where those who were doing this to him were hiding. He wondered, too, how his iPhone was receiving any service, but there it was: two bars of reception. An answer came to one of these questions. It turned out that Gallagher had not at all anticipated that John would keep his card: John was four digits into calling Gallagher when the recognition application tripped. The number had already been added to John's phone.

Gallagher answered after the third ring. "Tallinn *is* a nice place to spend a day. You should have listened to me."

What could John say? They had what they wanted.

"Nothing to ask? I don't blame you. You have bigger problems, Counsel. Right now you should probably turn around."

He did. Janika, on her feet and magically alive, hit John in the face with an instrument of formidable bluntness. When his knees met the carpet he saw the item clearly: the same air compressor he had used to beat the cockpit door. John's head turned mutant with pain. He did not remember the second blow but it must have come, because he awoke, once again suddenly, in a plywood room, tied to a chair. One of his eyes no longer worked. Some of his teeth were gone and his tongue felt as swollen and bloody and animate as a leech. He looked down at his shirt: a butcher's apron. The plane's engine was still in his ears. Turbulence shook the room. He could hear weeping somewhere close by.

Sitting across from John was Gallagher, whose hands were folded atop yet another sign. He did not show it to John, but John could read it. Gallagher told John he could promise questions but not answers. He told him this was new territory for all involved. Not even he was sure where this would go.

"Are you ready?" Gallagher asked. "I need to know if you're ready."

John nodded, covetous of his mouthful of blood. The door behind him opened. Footsteps. Hands like toothless muzzles took hold of him. Category V had begun.

Creative Types

The night before their appointment, they sent Haley one final email in which they reaffirmed the when and where and tastefully restated their excitement. But Reuben managed to smuggle in a request: Would Haley mind wearing "normal clothes"? He was about to hit Send when Brenna, proofreading over his shoulder, announced that his use of *normal* was, in this context, "problematic."

"Problematic," he said. Their son had been asleep for an hour.

Bren, looking at the laptop's screen, only nodded.

Reuben poised his email-sending finger above the Enter key like a scientist about to launch something toward Pluto. "Bren, come on. I'm sending it."

Bren paid this no attention at all, probably because she knew he wouldn't send it, not without her go-ahead. "*Normal.* It just seems like a very classist thing to write. Normal to *whom*?"

For as long as he'd known her, Bren had worried about classism. These days, of course, he and Bren were doing well, perhaps even embarrassingly well. However, their many years of doing less well had made Bren afraid of succumbing to the thoughtless consumption patterns of their friends, such as Annabelle and Isaac, who recently built a thirteen-thousand-dollar outdoor pizza oven with imported Umbrian stone. To Bren's way of thinking, success, particularly Hollywood success, was mostly an accident; she never wanted to condescend to those who hadn't been as lucky as she. But this meant that virtually everything Reuben said to servers and valets was later subjected to Bren's undergrad-Marxism rhetorical analysis. He didn't mind. If anything, he admired her for it. When Annabelle and Isaac whipped up their first batch of pizzas, everyone politely chewed and smiled on their sunlit patio. Bren was the first person to actually say, "Is it me or is this not very good?"

Reuben kicked back in his chair. "Well," he said, "you know what you're assuming, right?"

Bren looked at him. "What am I assuming?"

"You're assuming a woman in her line of work is automatically of a lower class."

"I am not." But as Bren thought about it, as he knew she would, her face fell. "Oh God. I am."

"And given her rates, I'd say that's a pretty dubious assumption, frankly."

Bren nevertheless convinced Reuben to put *normal clothes* in scare quotes, so "We'd appreciate it if you wore normal clothes (neighbors!)" became "We'd appreciate it if you wore 'normal clothes' (neighbors!)" Minutes after his no longer—or at least somewhat less—problematic email finally went out, Bren was rereading it on her phone. (She'd been cc'd.) "A *lot* going on in that sentence," she said unhappily. Haley's response came ten minutes later: emoji thumbs-up, emoji rose, emoji kiss.

Haley arrived the next night in a plain black circle skirt and kimonoish green blouse. She looked like the hostess of the type of sushi bar that had Mexican sushi chefs, so the outfit was normal enough, and already Reuben had a good feeling about how the night was going to go. This good feeling grew apace when Haley wrapped him up in a big tight hug. "It's so nice to see you again!" Haley said, her neck warm with spice and citrus, her hair a cascade of coconut, her clothes all powdered lavender. Reuben's hands were on Haley's back. They felt good there. They fit. Her blouse was satin, gem green, smooth and slick and glossy. Hugging Haley was like lying in a strange bed you didn't want to get out of. Then, beneath his hands, Haley's shoulder blades flexed; their hug was ending. Reuben stepped away, closed the door, and turned to see Bren standing in the long entryway hall, clasping her enormous wineglass by its stem. Haley moved toward her.

"Oh!" Bren said, as though Haley were a dirty-pawed puppy about to jump into her lap. "Okay! Hello!" While they embraced, Bren held her wineglass—a festive red orb of Malbec—up above her and Haley's heads, which somehow made Reuben think of mistletoe. His hands had been respectfully stationary on Haley's body, but Bren's free hand moved familiarly up and down Haley's back. That was one great sociocultural advantage of women's hands, wasn't it? They could go where they wanted to go. They had free rein.

Haley released Bren, after which she took up a position in the front hall that allowed her to look at both Bren and him simultaneously. She obviously wasn't in the habit of putting her back to people she didn't know well, and for that he blamed her not a bit. No one said anything for a moment. They were all smiling like naughty children.

"It's nice to see *you* again," Reuben said finally.

Haley laughed. "Ah. That. So when I arrive, I always say, 'Nice to see you again,' even if it's my first time somewhere."

At this point Reuben realized that Haley was subtly chewing gum. She had nice lips, and nice everything else, at least as far as he could tell. He wondered if he'd get to kiss her tonight. He and Bren had worked out some ground rules for what he could and couldn't do to Haley, but when it came to kissing, Bren was conflicted. It depended, she said, on how everything felt in the moment. What doesn't?

"Hey," Haley said brightly, "can I use your bathroom?"

Bren showed Haley the way. Reuben went to the kitchen and gulped down a swallow of red wine so large he was able to track precisely its journey from pharynx to gullet to gut. Around the corner from the kitchen area he heard the dull closing *thunk* of their upper-story half-bathroom door. Bren came back into view and mouthed, *She's pretty!* As though this were surprising. As though they had literally not gone shopping for Haley together. What surprised her, he guessed, because it surprised him, was how closely Haley resembled the lingerie'd human they'd seen in the jpegs on the escort website. Despite the check of authentication next to Haley's profile, they'd been preparing for the absolute worst on that front. Now he wanted to know: How did the site authenticate? Was there a lab-coated team driving around Los Angeles right now, skillfully authenticating escorts?

Bren approached and kissed him with warm parted lips. The Malbec and the Listerine breath strips they'd both been popping for the last two hours had not paired well, concocting a vaguely mephitine compound in their mouths. They'd agreed that the only way to do this was at least a little drunk, which was convenient. Since their son's birth fourteen months ago, they'd been spending a couple hours of almost every night at least a little drunk. Reuben couldn't remember the last time he and Bren had kissed like this, slow and tonguey and in no particular hurry. From the bathroom they could hear the compressed gush of their sink at half blast. Beneath the sound, Haley's voice maintained its steady murmur.

Bren pulled away. "Who do you think she's talking to?" She

was rubbing Reuben through his gray wool trousers the same slow way she'd been kissing him.

His hands were under her dress, rubbing her through her underwear, which felt like lacy braille stretched over warm moss. "I think they have check-in policies. Like, 'I'm here. If you don't hear from me again in an hour, call the cops.' "

Bren inhaled sharply; he was touching her just right. "Probably not the cops."

"Okay, not the cops."

Brenna stopped rubbing him, stilled his hand, and looked back at the bathroom. "I wonder if she's talking to her boyfriend."

Before Reuben could say anything, the bathroom door opened with its quick, efficient pop, and here was Haley, smiling, walking back into the kitchen area. *Please,* he wanted to tell her, *make yourself at home while I finger my wife.* Yet Haley somehow didn't notice he was fingering his wife. Instead, she set her carry-on-sized Hermès bag atop their granite-topped kitchen island and looked over the crackers, cheese, and olives they'd set out there. She smiled at the spread in a sadly amused way, like a woman who'd been proposed to by a man she'd just met. "Snacks," she said. "That's so *nice.*" (The snacks were Bren's idea. *It's not like we're hosting a dinner party,* he'd said, watching her lay them out. Bren's retort: *Company's coming. That means fucking snacks.*)

Bren began to rub Reuben through his trousers once again, but with faster, more performative gusto. This Haley noticed, saying, "Hel*lo,*" and putting an affectedly scandalized hand to her cheek. Interesting: he'd never been "watched" by a stranger doing anything like this before. In fact, the one prerequisite for doing anything like this was that a stranger *wasn't* watching. Being watched by this particular stranger turned out to be a lot more arousing than he'd anticipated. Haley seemed to think so, too. She actually steadied herself, for a moment, against their kitchen island. The snack tray was within reach, and for no reason Reuben could explain—maybe decadence was reason enough, for all of this—he reached out, secured a fat green olive, and popped it into his mouth. Salt, oil, brine: these were sex tastes. Probably why Bren put them out in the first place. Yet again, she was smarter than he was.

"Sooooo," Bren said, stopping to retrieve her wineglass, "do you need to ask us if we're cops or something?"

Haley crossed her arms and gave them a mock stern look of appraisal. "Pretty sure you're not cops. Also, it's a myth that cops need to tell you they're cops."

"Oh really? I didn't know that." Bren sipped her wine.

"I have a friend, a good friend, who met a client in his hotel room. This was, like, five years ago. In Hollywood. She sits down with the guy—good-looking, nice looking—and asks him, 'Are you a cop?' 'No,' he says. 'No way.' So she goes down on him. And he comes. And he arrests her anyway."

Bren, after a nearly literal spit take, said, "Wow," in a loud, flat voice.

"Obviously my friend is upset—"

Bren: "Well, *yeah*."

"—and says she'll narc him out. 'Who are they gonna believe?' he says. 'You or me?' "

"Not cool," Bren said. Meanwhile Reuben was thinking, *What happened to my hand job?* But Bren was locked into this conversation now. Processes of all kinds—and from all realms of legality—were of cardinal interest to her, and no wonder: Bren worked in unscripted television. She said to Haley, "So how do you deal with the cops? If you don't mind me asking."

Haley plucked from its dish a pitted black olive so wizened and oily it resembled the liver of a vampire bat. "Not at all! So what I do is I have a friend. She sleeps with a vice detective pretty regularly. He tips her off where the cops are gonna be that week. Which hotels. Like maybe it's 'Stay away from the W' on Saturday and 'Avoid the Roosevelt' on Tuesday." Thoughtfully, she ate her olive. "I prefer homes anyway. I really don't do that much hotel work. A lot of the entrapment rules were relaxed."

Bren: "Entrapment rules?"

"So yeah. Cops can get naked now. They can arrest you even if you just walk into the room in some places. Obviously certain states are better than others. California's actually okay. But if you have to get arrested, Hawaii's the place. They can't search your stuff without permission in Hawaii. Which is amazing. I got picked up in Maui once with three grams of pure Molly in my purse, and when I got out and got my purse back, I looked inside. Still there." She reached into her vaguely squarish Hermès bag, which really was a stunner, resembling an unusually elegant picnic basket. "Speaking of which." Now a white pill was pinned between Haley's thumb and forefinger; she showed it to them. "Do you mind?"

"That's Molly?" he asked.

"Yeah. I'll warn you, though—once I get rolling, I'm *very* friendly."

"Go ahead," Bren said encouragingly.

Haley stepped toward them. Actually, no. She was ducking under Reuben's arm, getting between them, squirreling herself right in there. Haley placed the pill on her tongue and closed her fingers around the stem of Bren's wineglass, just below Bren's fingers. She asked Bren, "May I?" Bren nodded. Haley guided Bren's glass to her lips and washed down the pill with a tiny First Communion sip.

And then Haley's hand was in Bren's underwear with his. "Do you have any more?" Reuben asked her, meaning the Molly.

161

"Sorry," Haley said. It sort of felt as if their fingers were oil wrestling inside Bren.

Bren was breathing hard; her hand was taloned around the knob of Reuben's shoulder. "We used to do coke," she said, between breaths.

Haley kissed Bren on the neck while the blood in Reuben's body began its vascular stampede. "Why'd you stop?" Haley asked her.

Reuben knew the answer: They quit doing coke because they'd had a baby, but Bren couldn't say that because they'd agreed they wouldn't tell Haley they had a baby. (The baby was staying with their nanny overnight, under the nearly accurate auspices of their need for "couple time.") They also wouldn't tell Haley that the whole point of this evening was to forget things like babies. They wouldn't tell Haley that, until they began seriously considering a night like this, with someone like her, they'd gone eight full months without having sex to completion, "to completion" being the operative term here, one or both of them having fallen asleep in the middle of the act on three different occasions. After they'd booked time with Haley, late last week, they'd had sex four times in five nights, though they wouldn't tell her that either. What else? They wouldn't tell Haley about the many times, before the birth of their son, that they'd privately mocked those couples with children who succumbed to literally knee-slapping laughter when asked if having kids had adversely affected their sex lives. They wouldn't tell Haley about how they'd reassured each other that their sex life wouldn't be so easily assassinated.

They certainly wouldn't tell Haley about the night, five years ago, when one of Brenna's on-set friends, Gemma, who was actually sort of Bren's subordinate (which: cue future problems) and going through a messy divorce, stayed late after a dinner party and somehow started kissing Bren, whose record of staunch heterosexuality had gone hitherto unblemished, which ultimately led to the three of them—Reuben, Bren, Gemma—groping on the couch and then retiring to the bedroom, and how this unsought but nevertheless astounding arrangement went on for a few weeks until Bren realized that Gemma, whose messy divorce involved drug use (hers) and infidelity (her husband's), was actually in love with Bren, or at least thought she was, and how after a couple weird incidents Bren told Gemma she felt obliged to report the whole sordid affair to their supervising producer, after which a duly mortified Gemma apologized and left the project, and how as upsetting as the whole thing was in the aggregate (the weird incidents included Gemma's seeming threat—feigned, thank Christ—that she'd recorded their *ménages*), what did Reuben and Bren go back to, what did they talk about and relive in so much of their sex that followed, including that which, he was pretty sure, conceived their one and only son? Of course, they talked about and relived those strange, silvery nights with loony Gemma and how utterly crazy they'd been for what they did to her separately and together.

The very last thing they wouldn't tell Haley was that they now understood why people with small children stopped having sex. It wasn't because they were tired or no longer attracted to each other, though that's what it often felt like. Intimacy between men and women begins as a hungry, prickly current that recharges itself by moving back and forth along a straight line. It was an *exchange*. But when you add a child to this line, it bends until it's no longer a line but a circle that goes past, through, and around you both, self-replenishing and internally regenerating. And this was a *process*. Once you've intimately bathed and dried and kissed your baby's knees and belly before bed and held your spouse afterward, perfectly and sexlessly content, the other, former, carnal intimacy—once so overridingly important—felt like nothing more than a low, disreputable road traveled in the dark.

Or: It wasn't possible for Reuben to read *Hippos Go Berserk!* twice in a row to their son and then go fuck Bren. Bren couldn't breastfeed and then return to bed and spread her legs for Reuben. Thus, Haley. Thus, this one night to walk again along the low, disreputable road.

"Drugs are fun," Bren said, in answer to Haley's question about cocaine. "For a while. Then you get old and discover Netflix." She leaned toward Haley to kiss her.

But Haley pulled away. "Let's take a little break," she said, removing her hand from Bren's underwear. "We've got plenty of time." This was true: they'd booked her for four hours. Haley walked over to the couch, removing her green satin blouse as she went and dropping it like a big shimmery lily pad on their hardwood floor. Tattooed on the small of Haley's back, in so-called tramp-stamp territory, were the words CLA$$Y LADY. Haley sat down, unhooked her bra, and patted the couch cushion next to her. "Come. Join me."

On her way to Haley, Bren took off her blouse, too, but left her bra on, so Reuben untucked and unbuttoned his shirt. They sat on either side of Haley, who gently took their hands and placed them on her breasts, which were small and warm.

"Sometimes," Haley said, "it's nice to get to know each other a little first."

"Totally," Bren said. She looked at Haley's breast in her hand and quickly burst out laughing. "I'm sorry, but this is just too funny." She extended to Haley the hand that did not have a breast in it for a quick shake. "I'm Bren, by the way."

"Haley," Haley said, shaking.

"So! What do you like, breast-wise? Should I squeeze or pinch or—?"

Haley put her hands on both their thighs and rubbed and kneaded. "Do whatever you like, so long as it's not too rough." Bren began to touch Haley with teasing lightness, which was the way she liked to be touched, at least initially; Reuben followed her lead. Haley, enjoying herself, or at the very least convincingly pretending to enjoy herself, made a vaguely feline sound and fell back against the couch cushion. "So tell me. What do you guys do for work?"

Bren and Reuben looked at each other. They'd talked about this, too—what to say and what not to say, in case Haley asked. They'd decided they'd just tell her the truth. She had their email, after all, and now their home address. That said, they couldn't imagine Haley actually would ask. But here she was, asking.

"I work in TV," Bren said, after which she started to kiss Haley's breast.

Haley smiled. "You and everyone."

"I know, right? We're everywhere." With that, Bren gave her a big wide-tongued lick.

Haley responded with a pleased shudder. "Oh really? Which show?"

"It's unscripted. A reality thing."

Haley's head swiveled over to him. "Let me guess what you do."

"Please don't."

"Okay." Haley was beginning to undo his trousers. Bren reached over to help: she knew the small, covered button on this pair of trousers was notoriously tricky. Unfortunately, Reuben was no longer hard. The culprit, he suspected, was Haley's CLA$$Y LADY tattoo, however small of him that seemed, and it did seem small of him. He knew it did. Reuben scooted away from their reaching hands. His hope was that if he stalled and watched them go at it a little more, his erection might return.

"Actually," he said to Haley, "now I'm genuinely curious. Go ahead. Guess what I do."

Bren stopped licking Haley's breast and looked at Reuben with smiling neutrality. He knew this look. It was her exactly-what-are-you-trying-to-accomplish-here look. She did not unleash this look very often, and the times she did it was invariably justified. Take now, for instance. Reuben in fact had no idea exactly what he was trying to accomplish here. Haley's arm was around Bren. But for the fact that Haley was naked from the waist up, one of Bren's pendulous breasts had escaped her bra, and Bren's mouth had recently been suctioned around Haley's nipple, they looked like tousled old friends spontaneously posing for a photo.

Haley carefully studied Reuben while playing with a strand of Bren's hair. "I'd say . . . you direct." Then she cunningly refined her guess: "Industrials."

"Ouch," Reuben said. "Also: no. Nice try, though."

But Haley had another guess in her chamber: "Then I'd say you're probably a writer of some kind." Bren laughed too hard too quickly. Haley turned to her for affirmation. "I'm right, aren't I?" Bren buried her nodding face in Haley's neck. She asked Haley how she knew. Again Haley looked at Reuben, her eyes less judgmental now, softer. "I don't know. He just looks like a creative type. You both do."

Reuben had published his first book, a short-story collection, at twenty-seven, three months after he'd finished his M.F.A. at Columbia, where he was widely loathed by his fellow fiction writers. Columbia was also where he'd met Bren, who was getting a master's in social work. Six months later, in December 2001, armed with fifty pages of prose and a febrile outline, Reuben sold a high-concept novel, a retelling of *Henry IV* set during the Soviet invasion of Afghanistan, in which a young Saudi fighter named Hassan has to contend with the influence of his stern, bin Laden–like father while an irreligious and overweight Afghan fighter named Fahad urges him toward a less violent life. The following spring, a PEN prize and a Whiting Award rolled in, after which Reuben set forth on the residency and fellowship tour—Bread Loaf, Yaddo, MacDowell, assorted European castles and estates—and occasionally worked on his Afghanistan novel. He never published his Afghanistan novel or, indeed, anything else. He taught briefly in Alabama and Virginia and finally moved to Los Angeles, at Bren's suggestion, to try his hand in the notoriously friendly and uncompetitive world of professional screenwriting. That didn't work out either. His longest-held job in Los Angeles was as a security guard for Barneys, which, he told himself, was research for a short story he never wrote. Happily, and totally accidentally, Bren found her calling in Los Angeles, lucking into a PA job on *Fear Factor*. From there she forged an actual career, working her way up from being a noted Hollywood sociopath's assistant to becoming one of three executive producers on *For Richer, For Poorer,* which took married couples of disparate financial circumstances and forced them to trade places for a week. In the landscape of unscripted, it was a show with an unbudgeable vision of civic morality, of *fairness,* a lot of which was directly traceable to Bren's influence. Still, three days a week, Reuben went to an office in West Hollywood ostensibly to write, and sometimes he actually did—sometimes he actually sat there and gave shape to airy nothings. He wasn't sure if Bren would be relieved or horrified to know that all he'd written for the last three years was poetry. Was it good poetry? Unclear. Really, how was he supposed to even know? Like any sensible person, he disliked poetry.

All of which meant Bren was the winner of bread in this particular household, Bren was the wearer of pants. Reuben didn't find the largesse of his generous, supportive partner emasculating or depressing—at least, it was no more emasculating or depressing than his failures as a writer. Often he thought back to the young writers whose careers launched simultaneous to his. He'd read with them at City Lights, had dinner with them at the American Academy in Berlin, done lines of pitiful coke with them at *n+1* parties in Brooklyn, and walked along foamy seasides with them in Saint-Malo. These days almost all of them were utterly and completely absent from what his former agent used to refer to as "the conversation," their sole published books selling for a penny on Amazon and their Wikipedia pages cruelly flagged for "notability." For a young writer, the most humiliating fate imaginable was to end up middle-aged and unnoted. As it turned out, this fate wasn't humiliating in the least. On the contrary, it was distressingly endurable. It didn't even hurt.

Maybe if Haley had asked Reuben what he did fourteen months ago, before the birth of their son, he might have said, with that familiar combination of pride and embarrassment, *Who me? Oh, you know. I'm a writer.* But his son was his world now, a living story he had all to himself, because Bren routinely worked seventy-hour weeks, whereas he was lucky if he worked a seventy-hour *year*. Reuben wondered, suddenly, what he and Bren were doing here with Haley when they could have been watching their son sleep or talking about him or sleeping and dreaming about him. Which is when Reuben knew. His boner had indeed been killed stone dead by Haley's CLA$$Y LADY tattoo.

"My turn to ask you something," Reuben said.

Haley and Bren were making out and touching each other, so her response was half spoken into Bren's mouth: "Go ahead."

"Your tattoo."

Haley stopped kissing Bren. They both looked over at him. "My tattoo," she said.

"Where'd it come from?"

She shrugged. "It's a tattoo. Where do you think it came from?"

"A tattoo parlor?"

Haley laughed and went back to kissing Bren. Bren's hand played along Haley's inner thigh before finally going for it. Haley's back went as straight as an icicle and she pulled Bren toward her. It was curious, how unbothered he was watching Bren's intimacy with another person. Earlier in his life, he'd been what was politely known as possessive. The older he'd grown, the more absurd behavioral ownership of any kind seemed to him. Fidelity was an insurance company, and roughly as reliable. Better to see the person you loved enjoying herself. He wondered if it would make any difference if Haley were a man. He didn't wonder long: of course it would. Bren had actually been in a threesome with two guys in high school. Here's how she described it: *No matter which way I turned, someone stuck a dick in my face.*

"It just doesn't seem very you, is all," he said to Haley, after a while. Her tattoo, he meant.

At this, Bren backed away from Haley and fixed upon Reuben a more burningly interrogative version of her exactly-what-are-you-trying-to-accomplish-here look. That's when Bren noticed her boob was hanging out of her bra. Almost shyly, she tucked it back in.

"Okay," Haley said. Although her voice was playful, her eyes had the flat, eerie calm of a storm-dark lake. "How is my tattoo not me?"

Over Haley's shoulder Bren was making an urgent new face, a face Reuben had never seen before. If he were forced to translate what this face was trying to communicate, he would have essayed something along the lines of: *Fix this situation you've created now immediately, you blundering fucking dolt.*

Reuben, taking Bren's point, put his hands up. "Haley, forgive me. If I've offended you—"

"You haven't offended me," she said quickly. "I'm—what did you say before?—I'm genuinely curious."

"I *like* your tattoo," Bren said with such obvious condescension she winced immediately after saying it. Haley didn't even bother to acknowledge her.

Reuben concentrated on holding Haley's gaze, which had grown colder by several centigrade. He tried to speak carefully: "It's just that your Hermès bag is, I think, ten thousand dollars"—the cost of women's luxury goods had always baffled and impressed him while he was working at Barneys—"and your tattoo, meanwhile . . . your tattoo seems . . ."

Haley stared at him with a sniper's malevolent patience while Reuben struggled with a respectful conclusion to his negative analogy.

"Seems like *what?*" Bren finally said when the silence became unbearable.

Reuben just shook his head. "I don't know."

Haley removed her arm from around Bren's shoulders. "Maybe," she said, "it seems like the opposite of a ten-thousand-dollar Hermès bag. Is that it?"

"Yeah," Reuben said. "Maybe." He watched as Bren's face tipped forth into the waiting platter of her hands.

For a moment Haley said nothing. Then she rose from the couch and walked over to the notorious Hermès bag itself. In went her fishing hand and out came an LG V10 phone, which she efficiently swiped awake. The startled light emitted by its oversized screen was so radiant the room instantly went from crepuscular monastery to lurid discotheque. After tapping in her code, Haley came back to the couch and sat. On her home screen was a picture of a younger Haley and another equally young woman. This other woman was brown-haired and less conventionally pretty than Haley, but taller, bustier, thicker, more sexually weaponized. The photo had been taken during or immediately after a night of vigorous partying: they both had greasy we've-been-dancing-for-hours hair and were throwing up fake gang signs. It seemed like a photo whose documentary survival absolutely depended on something terrible happening to the person in the photo shortly after it was taken.

"This is Vanessa," Haley said. "We ran away from home together and came to L.A. ten years ago, which is—God—kind of amazing."

"Why'd you run away?" Bren asked her.

"You've obviously never been to Moon Lake, Florida." Haley began cycling through other curated photos of her and Vanessa. Most had been snapped in nightclubs or bars. Compositionally, they were all the same photo. With every swipe, though, Haley and Vanessa grew thinner, blonder, harder, colder, while the backgrounds became darker and more frenetic. He could almost hear the ventricular music of these douche-bag pandaemoniums. After a dozen swipes, Haley said, "I found a place for us in Studio City, and we did the whole amateur-porn-circuit thing for, like, six months. Vanessa convinced me porn was a good way to get a modeling and acting career going. I was so stupid I believed her. See, I'm kind of a creative type myself. We made decent money for a while but spent it as fast as we got it. I really hated doing porn. The day I finally quit I had two scenes. First this guy comes in my eyes after I was promised he wouldn't. Then what

171

was supposed to be a girl-girl had the director trying to get in on it. He offered me twenty-five hundred dollars to go bareback with him, and that was enough for me. I walked away, discovered escorting, took some classes—"

At this Reuben couldn't help but interject: "Wait. Classes?"

"Courtesan classes. Led by an 'intimacy coach' who lived in Venice and made us refer to her as the Goddess. She taught me about posture, which is all in the shoulders, and about diction, and how to eat well, how to take care of my skin. I also took some personal-finance classes."

"From the Goddess?"

"No. Not from the Goddess. See, there's two kinds of escorts. The ones who do it because they choose to, and the ones who do it because they have to."

Bren: "And you're a Choose To."

"I am."

"Okay. Good."

"I tried to get Vanessa into escorting, but she liked porn better. It was faster, and she didn't have to take care of herself. It didn't really matter if she looked and sounded like a Moon Lake hick, because she was doing this gonzo hillbilly porn, so it worked for her. Some of it was really disturbing—incest, daddy's-girl stuff." Here Haley paused. "Which wasn't exactly healthy for her."

To this, Reuben and Bren said nothing. The screen of Haley's phone had become some kind of reverse Medusa: look away now and turn to stone.

Haley came to a photo of Vanessa wearing a spectacularly feathered white wedding dress. "Here she is getting married. Now that's a story. I was her bridesmaid. Check out her ring. Sixty-five grand." Haley slid the photo down and reverse pinched the screen to enlarge Vanessa's $65,000 ring, but all her enlargement did was exaggerate the pixilation: what was Vanessa's recognizable hand and ring at one moment became a smashed digital sculpture the next. "Her husband was an eighty-year-old widower from Vegas. They met on Facebook. His kids managed to block Vanessa with a prenup, and she wound up cashing out with something like a hundred grand. Of course, she didn't put it in a bank account because she didn't trust banks—don't even ask—and almost everyone she knew socially was a porn person or a crack dealer, so she couldn't ask them. I offered to introduce her to my financial adviser, but by that point she didn't trust me either. She was all messed up: meth, pills, coke. I do Molly, but that's pretty much it—other than weed, and only edibles. But drugs pushed Vanessa into some *crazy* situations. Like this one time, she goes to a party in Vegas and meets this guy, this rich Arab guy. At the end of the night, he asks her if she wants to go with him to Gabon, which is in, like, West Africa. Private jet. But there's a stopover first, in London. Vanessa thinks, *Great. I'll go shopping.* She gets twenty grand out of a hole she's dug in her backyard and flies to London with this guy. When she arrives she changes her twenty grand into pounds. But after eight hours in London the Arab decides they're going to Paris instead. Vanessa's like, 'Oh, okay,' and changes her twelve thousand pounds into sixteen thousand Euros. But they don't stay long in Paris either, and by this point the Arab is making her fuck every guy they meet. Eventually they get to Gabon. Vanessa's never been to Africa, obviously. It's not like I have, but even I'd know *not* to change sixteen thousand euros into six point eight million African francs. The Arab guy does whatever he does in Gabon— she's back at the hotel, fucking his friends—and they leave after three days. Vanessa lands back in JFK with six and a half million African francs, which no one—literally no one—in New York will convert back into dollars for her. The only way for her to get her money back is to fly to Gabon, change it, and come back to New York again. Which she does. She *still* doesn't know what she's doing in Gabon, so she gets ripped off, but to make a long story short she makes it back to JFK with a little under four thousand dollars—and she never even got to go shopping. The rest of her money she eventually spent on a new nose and boobs. My best friend, even when she stopped thinking of me as *her* friend, she was always my best friend. Before her head got all twisted, she'd do anything for anyone, if she could. Once, right after we first got here, I watched her give her last twenty dollars to a homeless lady. I asked her why—I was actually really pissed about it—and she said because the lady needed it more than she did. Which, you know what, was true. Last year, Vanessa finally wound up OD'ing on roxy, though I'm pretty sure it was suicide. There were only three people at her funeral."

Reuben and Bren were now looking at a photo of Haley and Vanessa as teenagers on what he gathered was a street in Moon Lake. Haley was wearing an *NSYNC T-shirt. Vanessa had braces.

"As for my tattoo," Haley said, "I got it on Hollywood Boulevard with Vanessa three days after I turned eighteen. I had other tattoos, a bunch of them, actually, but I got rid of them all. Lasers, followed by microdermabrasion. But I couldn't get rid of that first one, because it was Vanessa's idea. Her design even. It's a stupid tattoo and I hate it, believe me, but I couldn't do it. I couldn't burn it off. So I kept it, and when people ask—*really* ask, like you did—I decided I'd always tell the truth."

"Why?" This was Bren.

Haley turned off her phone. "Vanessa's family failed Vanessa and Vanessa's friends failed Vanessa and Vanessa obviously failed Vanessa. She let people rip her up and throw her away. So I use that. I use her memory to remind me why I'll never let anyone rip me up or disrespect me or make me feel shame. Okay? Like I said, I'm here with you because I choose to be. And I'll give you a great time. But I won't be shamed and I won't be pitied, so if you have any more comments about my body or who you think I am, I'd like to hear them now before this goes any further." That's when Reuben noticed that Haley's pupils resembled beads of dilated black oil floating atop her eyeballs. "And holy shit did I just start rolling."

"Would you like a glass of water?" Bren asked her.

"Absolutely," Haley said.

While Bren was fetching the water, Haley got Reuben's pants open, reached between his legs, and closed her hand around the formless squish there. She looked at him. "Everything okay?"

"I kinda lost it," he said.

"Well," she said, smiling, "let's find it."

Bren came back with Haley's glass of water. She sat down on the couch, still holding the glass, and watched while Haley went down on Reuben. Bren had the trapped look of a secretary with unpleasant news waiting for her boss to finish a trivial personal call. As for Haley's blow job, it felt no more or less erotic than being rinsed with a warm hand towel. When Haley finally stopped and looked up at Reuben, he could only shrug.

"Is there anything I can do?" Haley asked.

"I don't think so," he said.

Haley looked back at Bren, who handed Haley her water. She drank half the glass in one gulp. Bren, with a sad smile, said, "Incest porn—that's pretty much where you lost me."

Haley finished her water and set the glass on the floor. Her eyes were flicking everywhere, two water bugs trapped in the tiny ponds of her face. Thoughts seemed to tumble around in her skull's rinse cycle of drug logic, mismatched and unassociated. Finally, she stood. "All right. I've got an idea. Let's go to your bedroom. We can make this right." When Reuben and Bren didn't move, she grabbed their hands and pulled them up from the couch.

"Okay," Bren said. "Sure."

As they walked Haley to their bedroom, Bren held Reuben's hand tight. The three of them took off their clothes next to the bed in the sputtering light of fig-scented Diptyque candles, which Bren had set out earlier in the evening, right after she'd prepared the snacks, on the assumption they'd wind up here, doing exactly what they were doing. Haley began to kiss Reuben while Bren stood behind her with her hands on Haley's waist, but Reuben felt immaterial, like a shadow or a puppet. No, the shadows they cast on their bedroom wall were the puppets and they were the masters. Watch the black shapes move and intersect: they'd done this a thousand times. Above the stage, the puppet masters worked their puppets with one hand and read the obituaries and sipped coffee with the other. By this point Haley was rolling so hard that at times Reuben and Bren seemed only incidentally involved. Still, they tried any number of Modern Standard Porno positions: Reuben behind Bren on top of Haley, Haley on top of Bren while Reuben watched, Reuben on top of Bren while Haley watched, Reuben under Haley and Bren while they did whatever they were doing. Bren's moans were affectless, almost androidal: *Pressure applied and acknowledged, human.* Haley pursued her orgasm like a high-value bounty. She finally achieved it squatting over Bren's face while Reuben played with her breasts. When she was done, Bren crawled out from underneath Haley and went to the bathroom to wash up. Apparently, squirting was a thing Haley was capable of. Haley lay there on the bed next to Reuben, breathing and sweaty and glistening, a dessert he was simply too full to finish.

"I feel like you guys aren't having much fun," she said.

"Oh," Reuben said with an inflection that promised more words. There were no more words.

"We still have two and a half hours. Maybe it would help if you guys told me why you were doing this."

He could hear Bren peeing with the force of a garden hose in the bathroom and wondered how long she'd politely held it while waiting for Haley to climax. It was so like her, to do something like that. "We had a baby last year, and things since haven't been great, sexually. We thought this might help."

"Spice things up."

"Yeah. That was pretty much the plan."

"I get that a lot from the couples I see."

"I bet."

"Boy or a girl?"

"Boy."

"Name?"

"Theodore."

"That's a really nice name."

"We thought so. Classic, but not too common. We didn't want one of those L.A. baby names."

Haley breathed. Then: "I have a daughter."

Reuben bipodded onto his elbows to look at her. "Really?"

"Yeah. She's two. As of last week."

"What's her name?"

"Garland."

Bren was coming out of the bathroom and wiping her hands on a towel.

"Haley has a daughter," Reuben said. "Named Garland." Even in the dim light he could see Bren's what-the-fuck face. Quickly, he clarified: "I told her about Theo."

"Well," Bren said, climbing into bed, "I guess *that* cat's been debagged."

"I pretty much knew anyway," Haley said.

Bren spooned up against Reuben. "Really? How?"

"In the bathroom. Saw baby wipes on the shelf above the toilet."

Bren's small, appalled laugh was not without mirth. "Fuck. I remember thinking, *I have to move those.* Then I forgot."

"It's not a big deal," Haley said. "Is there anything else you guys want to do?"

Around the bed, strewn clothes, end tables, lamps and cords and phones. Beyond their bedroom window, the Hollywood streetlights were as bright as a forest fire. Even in the dark, all their things were illuminated and revealed. Bren rolled over and grabbed her phone from the end table. Then Haley did the same. Each already knew what the other was thinking.

"That's him," Bren said, handing Haley her phone.

"And that's her," Haley said, handing Bren her phone.

They said other things while Reuben watched one of Bren's scented candles burn down to the wick. Almost there. Wait for it. And there it was, the flame surging with a final valiant attempt at ignition. Then it went out. Then it waved its farewell banner of smoke.

The Hack

It would remain a subject of vigorous debate: How exactly did a hack joke wind up in James's *SNL* monologue when Sony had sent specific word *not* to make any hack jokes? A number of people wound up needing cognitive closure on the issue, which Daniel knew he was unable to provide. It was a shame, too, because everyone at *SNL* had been so nice. For Daniel, that was the most surprising thing. A few days ago, Wednesday morning, Kenan Thompson had given him a bleary-eyed hail ("Yo, D man!") as they were passing in the hall, even though Kenan had been up all night banging out sketches in time for the afternoon table read. He was pretty sure Aidy Bryant, Cecily Strong, and Bobby Moynihan all knew his name, too. The fact *anyone* had bothered to learn his name over the course of the week was unbelievable. Above and beyond. Especially when everyone had so much to do!

Long before he'd taken the job as James's assistant, when he was just a student at UCLA, his parents back in Wisconsin had warned him about what they called "slippery types" and "smoothies." Los Angeles people, they meant. *Hollywood* people. But after six exhilarating months working with James, Daniel couldn't even tell you what a "Hollywood person" *was* anymore. Most of the Hollywood people he'd met—and he'd met a lot— seemed like hardworking, sensible folks. (Daniel had learned that when you wanted to indicate a group of people apart from you, but whom you bore no malice, you called them "folks.")

Some Hollywood people were maybe a little intense or self-serious—yes, okay, fine. But here was the very important thing Daniel had learned working with James: talented people needed more *space,* psychically speaking. You can't crowd them or demand things from them, because they were always working inside their heads, even if it didn't seem like they were. Maybe that came off as aloofness to civilians—to the lame and untalented—but it wasn't. Not really. It took Daniel many weeks to figure this out, but once he did, his and James's working relationship really took flight.

Of course, the most exciting thing about working with James was everything Daniel got to see. Things so few people—his parents, his sister—would ever have the privilege to see. He'd been in and out of *SNL*'s offices all week, for instance, watching as the show went from some vague pitches on Monday to forty-six written sketches on Wednesday to twelve rehearsed sketches on Friday to nine full sketches today, Saturday (with one or more of those sketches likely to be cut by dinner break), that would finally be performed live tonight. Exciting! Daniel knew James was bummed that the businessmen sketch didn't make the cut; James told Lorne he wanted it, but he'd already gone to bat for the troll sketch, and Lorne, smiling, pointed out that not even hosts got to push everything they wanted into the show. Before they'd arrived in New York, James assured Daniel that he had a "good relationship" with Lorne. And he obviously did. After all, not many people could claim to have hosted *SNL* three times. Only two more and James was in rare company indeed, the Five-Timers Club, along with the likes of Bill Murray, Christopher Walken, Ben Affleck, Tina Fey . . . And yet Daniel wasn't so sure about the troll sketch. It seemed to him like James had (maybe!)

made a bad call. Cecily was *delightful* in it, as always—no one played a trashy white woman better, and Daniel, being from the upper Midwest, *knew* trashy white women—but the big shock of the sketch involved James making out with the adorable Kyle Mooney. Daniel knew he'd be hearing about *that* from his mother in Appleton, who now watched everything James did, and who in every conversation since Daniel became James's assistant burned up at least thirty-seven seconds with speculation on James's sexuality. "Just tell him to make a decision!" she'd say to Daniel, laughing. "Pick something and run with it!" She couldn't seem to grasp that James was goofing with his public perception, much less that nonbinary sexual identities were a thing now. Even when Daniel explained this, his mother still didn't get it. "Can't you just ask him?" she'd said the other day, with something like mania in her voice. "Can't you just ask him what he *is*?"

Daniel was beginning to sense his mother's emotional investment in James's sexuality went *way* beyond tabloid curiosity. But that was her cross to bear. *Sexuality* just wasn't the kind of thing he could talk about with James, even though he'd seen enough of James's private life to know that his romantic interests orbited Venus, not Mars. Even after six months—he'd never tell his mother this—there frankly wasn't *much* he felt comfortable talking about with James, despite Daniel being with him eighteen hours a day and controlling the passwords to his Facebook, Twitter, Snapchat, Gmail, Dropbox, iTunes, Instagram, Goodreads, LinkedIn, and Pinterest accounts, all of which passwords were different, never repeated, and changed week to week. He wasn't supposed to write any of the passwords down either. At first Daniel was confused. How in the living *heck* was he supposed to remember a dozen rotating, never-repeating passwords if he couldn't write them down? James could not have told you under pain of death what any of his passwords were but was adamant about this rule all the same. "Just come up with a system," James had said. "That's what Becky did." So Daniel had called Becky, who'd served as James's assistant before the Assistant Who Shall Not Be Named—he'd embezzled, which was bad, *and* sold James's clothing on eBay, which was way worse—and asked for guidance on this supposedly crackerjack password system of hers. Becky sighed wearily. Then the confession: "I wrote them all down." But Daniel knew that wasn't good enough, goddammit! And shame, shame, *shame* on her for deceiving James.

Daniel's system was this: he wrote down all the passwords in his iPhone, but as a simple Caesar cipher. (Thank goodness for his teenage interest in Alan Turing and World War II code breaking.) Obviously a Caesar cipher wasn't ideal, but Daniel was fairly certain the orangutans who sat in dark suburban basements while trying to hack their way into celebrity accounts would be blind to the tricky elegance of classical cryptography.

Then all this Sony business happened, this hacking *nonsense,* which was apparently in retaliation for the film James had made with Seth and which hardly anyone had seen yet. All of it was upsetting, for a host of reasons, not the least of which was the fact that a simple Caesar cipher was *exactly* the kind of code a properly trained hacker could break with one arm, cognitively speaking, tied behind his back. All he (maybe she!) would need to do was to crack Daniel's phone and peer remotely inside. When, a few weeks ago, news of the Sony hack first broke, very few understood how serious the matter was. Daniel included himself in that sad lineup. Initially, a few prerelease Sony films turned up on the torrent sites. Daniel, a little guiltily, watched one of them, which happened to be that Brad Pitt tank movie. It was the kind of soaring studio movie he loved yet hardly ever saw anymore, because he now saw movies only with James, who didn't watch studio movies unless he or his friends were in them, which was whatever.

These leaked movies were bad for Sony, obviously, but containable. Then, last Monday, the day James and Daniel had sat like schoolkids in the tight confines of an office on the seventeenth floor of 30 Rockefeller Center, surrounded by three dozen *SNL* writers and performers, a number of whom had apparently never heard of deodorant, listening to the pitches that later (magically!) became sketches, the salaries of Sony's top seventeen executives were leaked online, which his mother, for one, couldn't *believe* were pre-bonus salaries. Then came Wednesday, the night he got to watch the seasonal ignition of the Rockefeller Center Christmas tree, which was gorgeous and magical; Wednesday, dreary *awful* Wednesday, the hackers dumped into the internet's bottomless landfill yet another information payload, this one especially and viciously invasive, as it included, among hundreds of thousands of other things, a jpeg of poor Jonah Hill's passport. Jonah, who'd always been so kind to Daniel! James and Jonah had a long conversation about it, actually, because Jonah—who'd been one of the most vocal supporters of the Film since seeing the rough cut, singling out James's performance for especial praise—was pretty shaken up.

"Do *not* lose track of what's really at stake here," Jonah had told James, and Daniel agreed with that, too, even though Jonah, who was always so nice to Daniel, had yet to remember Daniel's name. During this call, on which Daniel had secretly eavesdropped while looking down from an empty office on the Rockefeller Center Christmas tree, Jonah went on to say that it was "more important than ever" for visible creatives such as himself to support the Film, even if that meant getting doxed, and Daniel pumped his fist in silent affirmation, because fuck, man, those fuckers—those lousy fuckers were anti-art, anti-expression, anti-everything-that-was-important (paraphrasing Jonah, obviously!). But Daniel *still* hadn't changed his Caesar cipher and he was feeling a little queasy-antsy about it, if he was being honest, and Daniel always tried to be honest.

Speaking of which: Daniel, too, had seen the Film. He didn't care for it. He didn't care for many of the films James appeared in, truth be told, but that didn't mean he didn't 100 percent support James's path as an artist and human being.

Friday, yesterday, was the first day he got scared. Someone or -thing calling itself the Guardians of Peace had sent an email to all Sony employees. Yes, they sent emails to the people whose access to email they'd nuked the week before, which was a stroke of tactical anti-genius on the so-called Guardians' part. In this email, they promised that "not only you but your family" would be in danger if they, Sony's employees, didn't append their names to an attached statement that denounced their employer in the most bananas possible terms. They also said this: "Many things beyond imagination will happen at many places of the world. Our agents find themselves act in necessary places." Of course, the Guardians' idiotic and ungrammatical message had gotten picked up and run everywhere to widespread mockery. But here was the thing that frightened Daniel: anyone stupid enough to regard those words as an acceptable threat on either a logical or a linguistic level was capable of infant-stomping, puppy-slashing cruelty. Stupidity was one thing and evil another, but evil stupidity? It had no focus. It was simply malignant, and you couldn't reason with that, could you.

James didn't seem that upset about the hack, oddly. Less upset than Daniel was, in any event. But then James rarely seemed upset about *anything*. Daniel knew that Seth, who was in more frequent contact with Sony than James, was handling it far less equitably. The Film was Seth's film, after all—well, Seth and Evan's film, technically—but as long as things cooled down, it would all probably be okay. The Film would be released, people would see it, the Guardians of Peace would stand down, and everyone could just move on. Daniel could keep his Caesar cipher intact and not have to manufacture another kooky password system to accommodate James's voluble social media presence.

Seth himself was due at *SNL*'s studio within the hour; he was doing a cameo during James's monologue tonight. Daniel was thus presently rushing out to grab lunch for Seth and James from the deli James favored whenever he hosted the august comedy institution. Daniel was in the middle of Sixth Avenue when he got a text from James, who was upstairs in his dressing room reading. This text was a *classic* James text. It said this: "Water." Translation: *Daniel, I'd like some water, please.* Daniel calculated how long it would take him to order Seth and James's food, wait for it to be prepared, and return to James's dressing room. Half an hour, at least, which was too long. So Daniel turned around, walked into 30 Rock, flashed his visiting VIP badge to the mountainous man in an ill-fitting blue suit standing sentry by the elevator bank, and rocketed up to the eighth floor, which was not the office floor but rather the studio floor, to which everyone had pretty much relocated as of Friday. He passed Kenan again coming out of the elevator but received no greeting this time, and Daniel tried to tell himself that this slight didn't bother him, even though it did.

James's dressing room was already jungly with the flowers of well-wishing friends. Supine on the stiff-cushioned couch—only partially visible through the orchids and lilies, like some fabled cryptid—was the man himself. He was reading *The Autobiography of Alice B. Toklas,* which Daniel knew was a novel written by the famous American lesbian Gertrude Stein in the purported voice of her lover, Alice B. Toklas. He knew this because, on the plane to New York, he'd asked James what the book was about. When James explained the book's conceit—books being one of the few things James seemed happy to discuss with Daniel—Daniel remarked that it seemed an oddly roundabout way to write about oneself. James had looked over at him with his crinkly-eyed smile, nodded, and went back to reading. Daniel knew he had somehow disappointed James, but that was okay, because he'd figure out a way to make it up to him later. That's what good assistants did.

While Daniel stood there in James's dressing room, he could see a large jug of icy water on the end table behind James's head. He could also see two bottles of Perrier poking greenly from James's sporty backpack. Daniel knew James could hardly have been expected to know that he, Daniel, was in the process of crossing Sixth Avenue when he, James, had texted. He further knew James wasn't precisely aware how much easier it would have been for him to get his own water, which was literally within arm's reach, *even if Daniel was in the next room,* much less rushing to beat a blinking red DON'T WALK signal in the middle of the Eastern Seaboard's busiest metropolitan area. Finally, and most important, he knew not to make an issue out of any of this. Two weeks after he'd first started working for James, he said something to him about the brusqueness of his beloved one-word text requests: "Water," "Apple," "Sandwich," "Keys," "Come," "Now." It seemed sometimes, Daniel said to James, it seemed sometimes like he was being yelled at by a robot. James's answer was simple: "You're my assistant. That's me asking you to assist me." Which, you know what, was an accurate assessment of the situation. But things add up, the little *injustices* of even a sterling working relationship, which he and James certainly had and which Daniel absolutely treasured. But things . . . well, they just add up. That was all Daniel could say.

He didn't speak to James as he fetched and gave him his water, which was, again, literally within James's reach, because right now Daniel could feel a wet, feverish heat behind his eyes. Daniel knew if he spoke, if he said *anything,* his voice would betray him. Then James would look at him, and put his book down, and ask if Daniel was all right, because James was always good about checking in when he sensed Daniel was upset, which Daniel was trying hard to be better about—not getting upset so often, that is—because James actually *did* care about his assistants' mental and physical well-being. Becky, for one, who claimed to love James for all his weirdnesses, had affirmed, many times, this very thing: "He *does* care. He's just busy. And you need to understand that you're not necessarily his friend. You *work* for him."

James accepted Daniel's Perrier hand-off without breaking eye contact with page 147 of *The Autobiography of Alice B. Toklas.* So Daniel turned and left James's dressing room. When he emerged from one of 30 Rock's deco elevators he felt a buzz in his pocket and already knew what James's text would say. It would say: "Lunch?" But it didn't. Instead, it said: "Thank you."

Daniel was still wiping tears from his eyes as he ordered James's double-decker tuna and Seth's egg salad sandwiches. When he finally returned to James's dressing room, Seth was already there, looking over the most recent draft of James's monologue. Seth held the loose, ardently highlighted pages with one hand while the other was plunged into his great brown nest of frizzy hair.

"Can't do this one," Seth said, looking over the lines. "Or

this one. Nope to this one. And no." He handed the pages back to James with the affect of a nurse disposing of used bandages. "They gotta rewrite this. The whole thing."

Sensing an opening, Daniel moved to hand Seth his egg salad sandwich. As he did, Seth glanced over at him and said, "Hey, Daniel." Even after six months, Daniel still felt a tingle that went as deep as his atoms when a celebrity of Seth's global influence—and absolutely no offense was intended here to Kenan, Aidy, Cecily, or Bobby—said his name aloud. Daniel coolly greeted Seth in return and handed James, whose face was scrunched up in confusion, his double-decker tuna.

James's focus remained entirely on Seth. "*Who* is this coming from?"

Seth, about to take a bite of his sandwich, stopped and lowered it. "Who do you think it's coming from?"

"Yeah, I get that, but why do *they* get to dictate *my* monologue?"

Seth set his egg salad back into its clear plastic container, where it seemed somehow even more tragic than an average egg salad sandwich. James's sandwich, for its part, hadn't yet been touched. In the elevator, Daniel had carefully inserted his finger into the messy labial fold of James's sandwich to check for sogginess. Maybe James liked the fact that his beloved midtown deli piled on twice as much tuna as was appropriate for the bread's load-bearing capabilities, but that meant the sandwich in question had to be eaten quickly, before the inevitable sog factor turned the bread into chowder. The longer these sandwiches went uneaten, the more ungainly (and unsightly!) a task eating them would become. It was all highly concerning to Daniel.

"Dude," Seth was saying, "they're not dictating *anything*. They're *asking* me to ask you to ask Colin and Rob to make sure nothing you say makes any of this worse."

Here Seth paused. And here James waited. They were extremely good friends, Seth and James, though they hardly ever hung out socially, which surprised Daniel's mom, for one, when he told her. James hung out with very few people socially. At night, all James did was read, write, and paint. Also, James was a teetotaler, while Seth's appetite for cannabis was nonpareil. Daniel wondered if they worked together so often only because it was the one way James could see Seth socially without feeling any gravitational pull back toward his weed-smoking, car-crashing teenage self.

"You gotta understand," Seth said, his voice soothing now, "things are really bad over there. *Really* bad. They're barely telling me anything and I can *still* sense how bad things are. Do you know how bad things have to be when someone's professionally obligated to convince you they're *not* that bad, and you *still* come away from the conversation thinking, *Holy shit, they're so fucked?*"

James laughed. Seth laughed. They sat there a moment, holding this buoy of mutually hopeless laughter. Meanwhile, the structural decay of two adequate but overstuffed sandwiches continued apace. "Yeah," James said. "Okay. I get it."

"They. Are freaking. Out."

James rubbed his face. It wasn't a gentle rub. It was a rough two-hander that ended with James pulling his sleep-starved eyes into slits. When he was done: "What I *don't* get is what else can they really do at this point."

"*They* Sony or *they* the shitbags?"

"The shitbags."

Seth fell back against his chair, weighed down by pondering the terrible enormity of such a thing. "I don't know. They've already tanked a bunch of their movies. Everyone's assuming they got emails. What happens if they release those?" Here, Seth popped back up. "Christ, you know how they talk. How *we* talk.

Amy and I went back and forth on the head thing and it wasn't fucking pretty."

The "head thing" referred to a scene in the Film in which the tritagonist's face explodes. It was a sensitive issue, as the Film's tritagonist was based on a real-life head of state regarded by his followers as having divine properties and whose strategic arsenal contained at least a dozen short-range nuclear weapons. The first cut of the Film, which Daniel had seen, depicted the tritagonist's exploding face in such exquisitely disgusting detail that the CEO of Sony, a man not prone to creative intrusion, objected to the sequence's gruesomeness. Edits were requested. It all became such a farce, Seth told James several weeks ago, before this hack nonsense, that he and Evan had pledged to digitally reduce the tritagonist's burning hair by 20 percent, 30 percent, and finally 50 percent, and went from claiming to need the explosion's secondary wave of head chunks to finally giving in entirely and obscuring the tritagonist's detonating face with smoke. Seth was undoubtedly right that the divulgement—the *exposure*—of such internally delicate editorial matters, so easily misapprehended, would not look good. For anyone.

"They're not gonna like it," James said after a while.

"*They* Sony or *they* the shitbags?"

"*They* the writers: Colin, Rob. I can't tell them to rewrite my monologue because it'll make Sony happy. What would *you* do, if you were them?"

Immediately, Seth smiled. "I'd tell every hack joke I could fit into seven minutes."

"Exactly. So would I."

Neither of them spoke for a moment. Then, Seth: "You want me to talk to 'em? Colin and I get along."

James sighed and, at long last, went for his sandwich. As Daniel feared, it began to fall apart the moment James had it in hand. James let the mess slop back into its clear plastic container, saying, in a tone of cosmic injury, "Goddammit." But Daniel was on it, handing James the plastic fork he'd secured precisely for this contingency. James accepted the fork and returned his full attention to his dear friend Seth. "No, man. Don't worry. I can do it. But we're gonna have to get Lorne involved."

Seth, too, began to eat, his response filtered through a muffler of egg salad: "Obviously, yeah."

Daniel imagined that the dressing room's triumvirate of odor—tuna, egg salad, pollen—was probably not the worst it had stunk across its many decades of colorful and differently accomplished hosts. Even so, Daniel's nostrils were troubled by a smell the word *stench* had been concocted to describe. He could have fainted were he not so otherwise attuned to the many, bewildering dependencies of the given situation.

While James forked away at the slop of bread and excess tuna in his clear plastic container, he read over his monologue for what had to be the thirtieth time. He smiled, and Daniel didn't blame him, for he'd read it, too, quickly, a few hours ago, while James was taking a call with his publicist. The jokes were funny; it was a really good monologue. When he was done rereading, James looked back at Seth with fresh consternation. "Not *any* hack jokes? None as in zero?"

Seth's hand lifted into Scout's-honor position. "Listen, I hear you. Loud and clear I hear you. But no. No hack jokes as in zero. That's what they asked for. As a courtesy."

"A courtesy." James's echo of Seth felt hollow and half-hearted. He then squeezed the bridge of his nose so hard that it looked to Daniel as though James were trying to hurt himself, which maybe he was. "Let's hope Lorne's feeling courteous."

—

Daniel tried to stay out of everyone's way for the rest of the afternoon, but he couldn't resist watching as the last of the sets—a dozen carpenters in the Brooklyn Navy Yard had been hammering and painting like madmen to finish them in time for the final rehearsal—were wheeled into the studio. Clothing was a major interest of Daniel's, which was something he had in common with James, who took even his T-shirt selection seriously. (Thoughtful T-shirt management was, in Daniel's mind, as good a gauge as any as to how much a man cared about his appearance.) Daniel had tried, as unobtrusively as possible, to hang around wardrobe a lot that week. This had been invariably challenging, given how frantically people were running about. It was mere hours before the final dress rehearsal now, which was always performed before a live audience. This, to better tease out what he'd heard one of the writers describe as a show's "dead spots."

Did you know that basically every *SNL* costume was held together with Velcro? True. That way, when the sketch was over and the cameras' red cyclopean lights went dark, the floor producer rushed over and just *ripped* off your costume, and off you went to the next set. These little stagecraft details were what Daniel most loved learning about. This is important: even though he'd taken James's creative writing class at UCLA, Daniel wasn't interested in being a writer. Not really. He was a communication studies major, not a creative. If he was being honest, and Daniel always tried to be honest, he applied for the class mostly because he thought it would be super neat to meet James in a classroom setting. While James hadn't been crazy about Daniel's fiction, he *did* respond to what he later described as Daniel's "fanaticism" for detail. James figured that meant Daniel would make a great assistant, and James needed a great assistant, especially after the embezzlement *debacle* with the Assistant Who Shall Not Be Named.

Now that he was here on the set of *SNL,* watching talented people work so hard to bring ninety minutes of joy and laughter to people like his parents and sister back home in Appleton, Daniel was just so . . . *happy.* The most interesting thing about Hollywood wasn't the acting or the writing. Noble callings, certainly, but not *interesting.* What kept productions moving, what made them fascinating, were the *details* people whose heroism needed no splashy credit, no outrageous remuneration. Unsophisticated people got addicted to Fun Hollywood, but Fun Hollywood was Dumb Hollywood. To master Real Hollywood was trickier, more intellectual. It was pure game theory. You had to read the people you worked with and wanted to work with. You had to understand professional microaggressions: when to use them, how to deflect them. You had to grasp that box office was nothing more than the hidden decimals of public perception. Real Hollywood was a game played alone, behind your eyes, second by thrilling second. It was chess and juggling and Dungeons & Dragons all at the same time, and woe to those who could not fathom this.

Which meant Daniel looked at what he was doing right now as work, plain and simple. Watching the Velcro pieces get fitted. Noting how the stagehands and writers matched cue card ink to performers, so there was never any danger of someone reading the wrong line. And even when Kenan Thompson, dressed to look like Rick Ross, came barreling toward him while yelling, "Yo, D! Get the fuck out of the way!" Daniel knew not to take it personally. Kenan was just being a performer; he wasn't seeing the whole picture. Still, Daniel was a little relieved when he received James's text ("Come lornes office"), because he would *hate* to know that his quiet, studious presence was making anyone's job harder than it already was.

Lorne had two offices. Daniel suspected, correctly, that James had meant Lorne's ninth-floor office, which overlooked studio

8H, where Daniel was presently decamped. That meant he was able to get up there within three minutes' time.

Lorne's assistant waved him into the room's creepy silence, which forced Daniel to analyze and read the situation he was suddenly stepping into. First, the obvious: Seth and James and Lorne were finishing their meeting with the head writers; almost certainly, this meeting was to discuss the necessity of scrubbing the (many) Sony hack jokes from James's monologue. Daniel later learned that this meeting had gone really well. The writers accepted that they weren't being asked to defer to some ridiculous PR request but were rather being asked to contain an act of sabotage in the reciprocal spirit of enlightened industry colleagues. However, one of the writers (Daniel never found out who) suggested including a hack joke that wasn't actually *about* the hack—i.e., not a joke at Sony's already battered expense. Instead, it would be a hack joke *at the expense of Seth and James*. That was when Daniel entered Lorne's office, in the nano-moment immediately after the hack-joke-not-actually-about-the-hack had been pitched. Daniel had been in enough meetings now to recognize that dense, hanging, post-pitch moment, in which everything went silent, and which always felt to Daniel like those terrible few seconds in Little League when a fly ball had been punched out toward him in right field, wherein he always had *just* enough time to reflect on the unlikelihood of his actually catching the ball, not to mention the various social cruelties that would befall him if he didn't catch the ball. (He never caught the ball.) So while Daniel didn't get to actually hear what this newly pitched non-hack hack joke amounted to—the content of it, that is—he *could* tell that Seth, for one, was skittish about the whole thing.

"I don't know," Seth said, stretching out each word, looking not at the writers but rather staring at the carpeted floor of

Lorne's office. With Seth so distracted, the three head writers traded quick pack-hunter glances; they wouldn't push any harder than this, but Daniel sensed how dearly they wanted to. Lorne, a saturnine presence in his leather power-executive chair, watched Seth deliberate. Lorne was getting older, bulldoggier, but he was still handsome, and his brushy haircut, dabbed with the perfect amount of product, was superb. Glasses, a Dunaway-folded pocket square, and was that an Armani *jacket*? Give it up: the man had style, unlike his writers in their Levi's and indifferent buffalo check flannels. This was Daniel's most intimate contact with Lorne, "intimate" = standing within fifteen feet of the man while remaining moderately certain that he knew who Daniel was and roughly why Daniel was there.

Lorne occupied a particular entertainment-industry crag, one that Daniel had long seen as ideal for someone like himself. Not a captain of men so much as a wrangler of men. Not a talent but a dowser of talent. Not a famous name (not a name his mother would necessarily recognize) but a notable presence among the famous—someone they all respected and deferred to. Daniel could tell just by watching Lorne interact with his writers that he didn't *need* to say anything beyond no. No justifications, no explanations. If Lorne didn't like it, it wasn't going forward. Holy cow did Daniel admire that. He longed to live his life in such a creatively integral way, with such a track record.

James stood before and looked out of Lorne's inward-facing office window, which allowed a clear view of the doings down there on the floor of studio 8H, where in a few hours' time millions would watch James perform his monologue live. When he turned and noticed Daniel's arrival, he walked soundlessly across the room and pulled him aside. "Do me a favor." James's voice was low. "Have Deon call Sony and find out if we can do one hack joke at our own expense. See if they'd mind." Deon was James's production partner, as well as the man in charge of Daniel's compensation, invoices, and performance reviews.

Daniel tried not to respond too eagerly, even though this was *exactly* the sort of task he excelled at. Passing oblique messages too sensitive for texting. Serving as a conduit. Working behind enemy lines. Daniel had no wish to disturb the monastic silence of Lorne's office, so he typed the following into his Notes app and showed it to James: "Who am I telling d to call?"

Again, James spoke quietly. "He'll know."

As Daniel was leaving, he heard Lorne tell an increasingly agonized Seth, "I can get Amy on the phone right now and clear the joke. That's easy." Daniel stopped, knowing that if Seth agreed to Lorne's request to call the enviably well-regarded Amy Pascal, chairperson of Sony's Motion Pictures Group . . . well, that made Daniel's mission moot. James surely knew this, too, and he stood there by the window, behind Lorne, with one hand subtly lifted, as though holding Daniel in place with nothing more than brain magic.

But Seth shook his head. "I don't wanna bother anyone there right now. Especially Amy. I *really* don't. It's the last thing she needs."

"I'll call Amy," Lorne said, but Seth didn't respond. So James gave him the go-ahead. Unambiguously. Daniel left the office and immediately called Deon, who didn't pick up, who *never* picked up. He then texted Deon a simple follow: "Call me." At which point Daniel received a text about one of James's upcoming film projects, a location issue that required Deon's approval, which Daniel immediately forwarded to him. At roughly the same time, as Daniel later learned, James and Deon were texting about an unrelated matter, and James asked Deon if Daniel had been in touch. Deon, believing James to be referring to the location issue Daniel had just forwarded him, and which he immediately approved, texted back, probably a little too ambiguously, "You're good." Which meant James believed he had approval from Deon's contact at Sony. James then relayed to *SNL*'s head writers that they could go forward with the gentle, self-mocking hack joke that was already taking shape, and which required Seth and James to (among other things) appear nearly naked in a raunchy mock-up of a Christmas card photo. Meanwhile, Seth apparently believed Lorne *was* going to call Amy Pascal and get approval on *that* end. That never happened either, which meant a systemic failure at multiple junctions. It wasn't his fault.

When the monologue was finally performed, and did really well, a few hours later, before the test audience, everyone from Lorne to the writers to Seth and James thought they were good. They'd acknowledged the so-called elephant in the room and managed to do so in a way that did not sully the honor or reputation of Sony, its subsidiaries, or its employees, who by now had been through so much. True, Daniel could have extended himself and made sure Deon put in James's requested call to Sony, but after the meeting in Lorne's office Daniel's day began to go very, very fast, and to be perfectly honest he forgot about it. The paradox of being so detail-oriented was that you simply had *that* many more details to keep track of! Of course, the enormity of the problem did not become apparent to Daniel until the live performance itself, when he was sitting in the green room, watching James's monologue on one of the monitors with various friends of the show and other VIP guests.

And there Seth was, sauntering out into James's monologue to giddy whistles of audience approval. And there *they* were, James and Seth, best friends, standing together, nervously discussing the hack, which impelled James, as per the joke's setup, to announce his preemptive disclosure of everything currently on his phone. This included photos of him sitting on a toilet naked, curled up with Seth in a parody of a compositionally similar photo of John Lennon and Yoko Ono, and the aforementioned raunchy Christmas card photo, all of which the audience responded to warmly—but not as warmly, Daniel noted, as the test audience had.

The broadcast version of the show was, of course, on a seven-second delay, and it took the passage of those seven damnable seconds for Daniel to realize that Seth's phone, which had been left on the chair beside Daniel's, was lighting up despite having been set to mute. Daniel recognized the senders' names of several incoming texts, and he *certainly* recognized Amy Pascal's name when her call inevitably filled Seth's screen. It wasn't at all clear to Daniel what he could or should have done at that point. Obviously, when Seth returned to the green room, Daniel smiled and pretended he hadn't invaded Seth's privacy by quickly, secretly scrolling through half a dozen angry texts. Seth began to scroll through the texts himself, saying only, "Oh shit." Daniel focused intently on the green room's monitor, where James was doing a sketch in which he somehow played Christopher Walken playing Captain Hook, and which was sinking, as Daniel's accountant father liked to say, like a submarine made of turds.

It was extremely painful for both Daniel and James to have to spend such a large portion of the show's after-party sitting in the back of Dos Caminos while James asked Daniel to walk him through each step of the process by which he and Deon had gotten their signals so calamitously crossed. They were in a booth latticed front and back with yellow wood, which made it feel like an unusually festive prison cell. James sat across from him, arms folded, while Daniel sat with his hands in his lap, his knee amphetaminically bouncing.

Daniel didn't mean to start crying—he never *meant* to start crying—but part of him also knew it was the quickest, most efficient way to get James off his back, because James, as established, really *did* care about his assistants' mental and physical well-being. So many of James's assistants had gone on to do *marvelous* things, and Daniel had every intention of following in their hallowed footsteps. Obviously, that would be easier if he had a good recommendation from James, so it was very much in Daniel's interest to keep their sterling working relationship intact. And if it took bountiful weeping after an innocent mistake that got James's best friend yelled at for thirteen minutes by the chairperson of the American subsidiary of a powerful global entertainment brand . . . well, that was what it took. No apologies.

But James surprised Daniel by *not* backing off. If anything, he *bore down*. "Daniel," he said, his irritation unmistakable, "you can't cry every time you mess something up. For one thing, it's *extremely* off-putting. Sometimes I need things to get done, and you're not doing them. It's really . . . it's just incredibly frustrating sometimes."

"I know," Daniel said, aware that several people from the cast and crew (most holding engine-coolant-colored margaritas) were looking over at him and James and the utter *scene* they were making. "I'm so sorry. I'm trying to do a good job."

A look of concern passed over James's face, after which Daniel repeated the version of the story he had actually come to believe, which was that he and Deon had a quick conversation about Deon's need, as per James's request, to call Sony. It happened. It totally did. He could almost remember their imaginary conversation. Word for word.

James's face hardened. "Right. The problem is Deon's telling me that conversation never took place. So I'm stuck thinking one of you is lying, and I have my suspicions about which one of you is."

"Deon's *not* lying," Daniel said desperately. "It was a really quick conversation, the reception inside the studio was horrible, and he and I had at least *four* conversations today about various things." Helpfully, almost all of that was true. "I *thought* he'd understood what I said to him, but I guess he didn't. It was just a miscommunication. I'm so sorry. Don't blame *Deon*." Daniel remained quiet for a moment. Then he asked if Seth was all right.

James's small, humorless laugh was a puff of desert air. "Yes. He's fine."

"It's just that I heard the way Amy was *yelling* at him—"

"Daniel. Seth's a big boy. And that's not the issue. The issue right now is that I don't know if I can trust you."

Daniel made sure his eyes were dry and he was sitting up straight, his shoulder blades pulled back, when he told James in his most unwavering, least uptalky voice, "You can trust me. It was a miscommunication. That's all."

James fixed upon Daniel what he could only describe as a richly conflicted look, his mouth a grim slot and his eyes soft with pity. It was a suspicious look and a confused look. It was the look of a man who had no wish to append another problem to a problem. It was the look of an artist who just wanted to do his thing and not have to worry whether the person to whom he sent an average of eighty-seven texts a day was trustworthy or reliable.

Behind James, deep in the restaurant, Cecily Strong was dancing in the goofy loose-armed manner of someone who would sleep until 4:00 p.m. tomorrow, while the writers who did not perform tonight, who had no real way to exorcize the cumulative tension of six straight days of work, stood around, watching her dance, their faces hanging and sallow. These were refugee faces of people who'd struggled to do something, get somewhere, and who now had to wonder whether it was worth it, whether they really were where they wanted to be. For his part, Daniel was *exactly* where he wanted to be, even if that meant getting yelled at.

James uncrossed his arms, and Daniel, sensing what was next, let himself unclench. See, James just didn't know—had no idea—how hard it was to do what Daniel did for him, day after day after day. So Daniel was glad for moments like this, moments in which Daniel could let James know just how *hard* he worked for him. How *much* he cared.

"Okay," James said. "Just . . . keep trying to do your best. All right?"

"Of course," Daniel told him.

"We're off tomorrow," James said, rising, "but we have Stern on Monday. So take it easy. Go to a museum or something."

A *museum*? Did James really know that little about Daniel? Possibly. Probably.

What was so *frustrating* was that Daniel was trying to *help* James! See, when someone or something like the Guardians of Peace came at you, blades drawn, it was *never* people like James or Seth or Amy Pascal or even Lorne standing at the front line. It was foot soldiers like Daniel. They knew what the stakes really were, the color and texture of every ugliness liable to gush from punctured, famous lives if the Guardians attacked again. Almost certainly they would. But Daniel would stand firm. He'd protect those who couldn't protect themselves. See, being famous didn't make you smarter or special. Fame was just a magic trick. That's all. It moved invisibly through our world and just kind of landed on certain people—some deserving, some not. But everyone had the right to a small corner of anonymity, a place in their lives where they could be nothing better or worse than themselves.

Daniel watched as James was welcomed back into a throng of *SNL* people with congratulatory hugs. He watched Kyle Mooney's mouth form the words *Great show, man!* and Cecily Strong ask, *Is everything okay?* while trying and failing to keep from glancing over at Daniel. Smart woman, Cecily Strong. Perceptive. But just a performer. She had no power over Daniel. Not really. And someday he'd have power over her. Not that he'd *ever* misuse that power. But he'd be aware of it. The best part? So would she.

Acknowledgments

Thank you to editors Sven Birkerts, William Pierce, Heidi Pitlor, Geraldine Brooks, Ted Genoways, Owen King, Otto Penzler, Jeffery Deaver, Steven Church, Stephen King, Bev Vincent, Oscar Villalon, Bill Henderson, and Ben Fountain.

Thank you also to Heather Schroder, Dan Frank, and Andrew Miller, who have shepherded and supported my work for nearly twenty years now.

Thank you to Dan Josefson and Adrienne Miller, who read all of these stories multiple times, and whose suggestions to improve them were invariably correct.

Trisha Miller is why I write. And for that, she has more than my thanks. TLM, I love you more than words can wield the matter.

A Note About the Author

Tom Bissell was born in Escanaba, Michigan, in 1974. He has been awarded two Pushcart Prizes for his short fiction, and his previous story collection, *God Lives in St. Petersburg,* won the Rome Prize from the American Academy in Rome. Two of its stories, "Expensive Trips Nowhere" and "Aral," were adapted into feature films by directors Julia Loktev and Werner Herzog. He has also published eight works of nonfiction, including *Apostle, Extra Lives, The Father of All Things,* and *The Disaster Artist* (with Greg Sestero), which was a *New York Times* best seller and adapted into an Academy Award–nominated film. He currently lives in Los Angeles with his partner, Trisha Miller, and their daughter, Mina.